I0739260

A Sad Saga

In 1940's

America

How a ten-year-old boy perceived events…

By

Robert Snow Wiltshire

Edited by: Susan Seawolf Hayes, Lynn Perretta, Sybrina Durant and Marissa Elliott

Tributes by: Regina Ramsey and Marissa Elliott

A Sad Saga of 1940's America

How a 10 year old boy perceived events....

Copyrighted 2015

Paperback ISBN-13: 978-1508995609, ISBN-10: 1508995605
Ebook ISBN-13: 978-0-9960940-8-5, ISBN-10: 0996094083
Paperback ISBN-13: 978-0-9906537-9-0, ISBN-10: 099065379X

BISAC Codes:
FIC000000 FICTION / General
FIC002000 FICTION / Action & Adventure
FIC008000 FICTION / Sagas

All rights reserved by Sybrina Publishing and Distribution Company.

League City, Texas, United States of America

This book contains material protected under International and Federal Copyright Laws and Treaties. Any unauthorized reprint use of this material is prohibited.

No part of this book may be reproduced or transmitted in any form or by any means, electronic or mechanical, including photocopying, recording, or by any information storage and retrieval system without written permission from Sybrina Publishing and Distribution Company.

Contact Sybrina@sybrina.com.

Table Of Contents

Ch. 1: Morley Owns A Special Horse

That Morley's horse was very special and *just how* she was very special will not at first be evident but will become so as we continue our story. For one thing, right off, she was completely blind in the left eye and near blind in the other. She was old as well - so Morley said anyway.

One thing I learned about her very quickly, to my dismay, was she would not let just anyone get on her back...like me, for instance.

She was the first horse I rode, although, quite naturally, I knew nothing about horses. I think she knew it and just decided it was time to be more particular about who was going to ride her. Her way of serving notice about this was through her treatment of me.

Even though Morley said it was all right for me to get on her, it seemed that he forgot to ask Myrt about it. Her name was Myrtle, but everyone just called her Myrt for short. She almost dragged my left leg off on the side of a grain silo, and the scream I let out pretty well got the message across:

By Yiminyi, that hurt!

Fortunately, no permanent damage was done, but I quickly developed a healthy respect for horses and things of a like nature. From that day forward, any thoughts I might otherwise have had about becoming a jockey were dashed once and for all.

Incidentally, that was the first but not the last time I would have to mount her on the wrong side. The second and last time I did, thank Heaven she seemed to understand that it was an emergency and she let me get by with it.

On the first attempt, I like to have never got up in the saddle. Myrt just kept going round and round, and I could not get my leg over. Morley, who I would later have good reason to believe was certifiably crazy, was yelling something I could not make out. It sounded a lot like he was calling either Myrt or me a very bad name.

When I did finally manage to get my leg over the saddle, she quit going around, took off, and made a straight line for this metal silo. I thought she was going to hit it head-on, but she only grazed it on her blind side. It was enough nearly to tear my left leg off! That is when I yelled out with that bloodcurdling scream - and you can pretty well imagine that it more or less took the edge off the other planned festivities, at least for me.

Well, this was most unfortunate, coming as it did on what was to be a very special occasion for my family and me. More so for my mother, for we had been invited to dinner at the home of her childhood friend. The two friends had not seen each other since their freshman year in High School, more than fifteen years past.

Many things had changed since her school girl days. Mother had married my father, and her friend had

married a man by the name of Mitchell - Denny
Mitchell, to be exact. Denny Mitchell, father of Morley
Mitchell, is who this story will be about.

Mother had married a poor hard working farmer. He was
a good and honest man who toiled long days and hours
as a sharecropper for wealthy landowners. In this case, it
was only 80 acres out of thousands, owned by the Great
American General Land Company.

From this farming effort, we had to pay half of whatever
we earned to the land barons as their share of the profit
from our labor. That was in return for their letting us
live in a small 4-room, tin-roofed wooden house.

*It was a hard life, and there was just barely a living that
could be made, even if we did get in a good harvest in
the fall of each year, which unfortunately we did not
always manage to do on account of too much rain or too
little rain.*

Then there were the floods that we had to face since we
lived between two great rivers, one being the St. Frances
and the other being the Mighty Mississippi. This was in
the days when the levies of each were not able to hold
the enormous amounts of water added to them in times
of extended rains. It seemed to us like these great rivers
broke their levies about every third or fourth year.

Still, we lived in and farmed the rich bottomlands that
made up the deltas of these two dominating rivers. Thus
when we were able to gather a crop, it was usually a
banner harvest.

We were able to pay down on our debt to the company-owned store; and once, I believe we came out even. We got out of the red and into the black. But alas, we never stayed there for long.

While we were not vassals out and out, ours was certainly not a case of *to the manor born*. Since we could not get out of debt, our prospects for getting ahead were slim to none, and slim was always sickly and finally up-and-died, if you can follow my meaning.

Then quite by accident, Mother happened to meet up with a childhood friend, who it turned out was now married to a man we all knew of. We had never met his wife, but he was by all local standards, obviously, very successful. He owned several hundred acres, though most of it was low-lying and swampy. It was forested by thick timber which was in turn almost impossible to hunt through on account of there being so much heavily tangled undergrowth. It was more like a jungle than something one would expect to find in Southeast Missouri.

More about this tangled oddity later. Now I must return to that memorable visit the family Wiltshire made to the home of Mr. and Mrs. Denny Mitchell, Mother's lady friend, whom she had not seen since high school days some 15 years past. Remember?

We got all dressed up for this event, and my mother let it be known that this was going to be a very special visit, so we, that is - my brother, my sister and me - had best be on our very best behavior.

It was understood that if something did go wrong, you could bet that in some way I would be involved. Who knew that something as innocent as me getting on that old blind horse – agreed, on the wrong side – would make old Myrt act up so in spite of all my efforts to stay on that she'd reward me by almost killing me? How absurd could that be?

I have always believed Morley knew.

It pretty well took the skin off my left leg. All the grown folks thought that while it did look bad, in time it would heal. They believed there would always be some noticeable scarring.

Since I was a boy, they figured that was not as important as it would have been if I had been a girl.

I thought, Now how do you figure that?

Ch. 2: My Leg And Pants Part Company

I was only ten at the time. Anyway, as for my khaki pants, well they was ruined for the most part – plumb ripped the left pant leg off my new britches. As for my injured leg, they brought out some purple liniment and a dauber – a small mop – to apply it. They doctored me up right there on the spot – the spot being there on the back porch – where whoever wanted to could and did get a free peek while they daubed me up.

The only thing that kept me from screaming from the pain was that heavenly vision through the open window. There in the window, I could see that large bowl of banana pudding just setting there, waiting for all this to be over so I could set about some serious eating.

That was the main reason we had come here to begin with - it for sure was not for me to be nearly killed by Morley's old blind horse. Now, I was to be further humiliated by them stripping me half-naked there on the back porch. That was how it seemed, at least, when I had to drop my pants for a better examination as to what extent I was hurt.

Anyways. I was not wearing no BVDs, if you know what I mean.

Well, to tell you that our visit had got off to a bad start would be putting it mildly. At this miserable point in time, Dad was making threats as if to leave the

Mitchell's fine abode and immediately cancel all of the festivities in store. Mother was embarrassed and on the verge of tears, and she was doing her best to disguise her worries about me. To make matters worse, Mr. Mitchell thought he could restore our merriment by killing the horse!

To have done so – take care of that horse – in those days would not have been as out of character for certain men as one might think.

I am certain that Mr. Mitchell's questionable son, Morley, knew this because he became noticeably agitated. He exuded fear bordering on hysteria as he ran out and got on old Myrt and took off. This sent everyone running after the rogue duo.

I thought it strange that Myrt would do right for Morley, but she would have nothing to do with me. Then I realized I was alone, just old pudding and me. Now was the time to make someone pay for my ordeal. I felt that Morley had set me up. I felt sure he knew what old Myrt would do with someone strange on her back, because he had laughed.

In this and other ways, he was a strange duck. I simply attributed it to him being an only child, but I did not appreciate him snickering at me, especially when he pointed at me while referring to what he laughingly called my "short fall," if you will, pardon my figure of speech. He was making a smart remark about how I was caught with my pants down, smarting off in other not so subtle ways. I was beginning to care less for this Morley

Mitchell.

I started to suspect that the boy was not right.

Anyway, after I pulled up what was left of my pants, favoring my skinned up leg, I hobbled over to the table where Mrs. Mitchell had sat this great big unguarded bowl of banana pudding. No picture ever looked as good to me as this dessert, made by Mrs. Denny Mitchell. Though I was sorely tempted to claim this one for myself, I managed to hold off. Things were bad enough as they were. An act of this nature would have put things completely out of reach, as far as trying to restore a happy time for all of us was concerned.

It was about then that Myrt showed up without Morley. Dad came running up, alarmed and out of breath, shouting for me to ride to go get old Doctor Spears. It seemed that Myrt had thrown Morley over her head when she slid to a sudden stop. She had refused to make the jump he had required from the wooden bridge that spanned one of our several large floodway ditches. They say ditch, but it was more like a small river, though there was no railing on any of these bridges, four in all. Even for a young horse, this would have been near impossible and while the water was deep, the remains of some dead tree trunks could be seen, which made it all the more dangerous.

It looked as though Morley was trying to kill himself along with his beloved horse. I suppose he could not stand to lose Myrt by his father shooting her, especially over something that wasn't her fault. I could certainly understand this, as I felt the same way about my recently tore up leg, not to mention my new khaki pants. Not old Myrt's fault, those things that happened; not my fault my leg and new khakis got tore up.

I was being asked to ride for help on an old almost blind horse that I had every good reason to believe would not even let me get back in the saddle. Even if she would and I could, there was still a hard ride to be made with a bummed up leg. All this, for someone that I was fast developing a rather healthy dislike for. Why, it was only about a half hour before that Mr. Mitchell's only boy was having some good sport at my expense. Now he was lying down there under one of those bridges needing my help.

Was I going to help him?

Well, it was the right thing to do. In addition, my Dad had asked me, forgetting about what had happened earlier. A boy needed help. He might be hurt, and caught on brush above the water. Dad was going back to do whatever he could to help, and needed me to be careful and hurry.

Then I had an idea that would serve two purposes if it worked. I hobbled into the house, made it to the kitchen table, grabbed that banana pudding, and carried it outside to see if Myrt would eat any if I offered it to her. If she ate any of it, then I would too. If it became necessary, I would blame it on the horse.

Ch. 3: The Proof Is In The Pudding

Would you believe she did eat that banana pudding? She seemed to go for it, especially the Vanilla Wafers more so than the bananas. I spent several seconds feeding Myrt what I felt was really my pudding. I became so interested in watching old Myrt go for it that I forgot about my original, sinister intent. Then I realized that I had waited as long as I could, probably longer than I should. I managed to get back in the house, found a spoon, and smoothed out the pudding so that maybe no one would notice right off that any was missing. After I got it looking as good as possible, I limped back out to Myrt, and finally tried to get into the saddle, on the left side this time. That was the right side after all.

She let me and after I petted her a little, I said, "Let's go girl. Seems like your buddy needs our help. Let's go get old Dr. Spears, and maybe he'll come out here in that new Model-A Ford of his." It was yellow and black and sure was pretty to look at.

"Would you like that?" At which old Myrt looked around at me, and then for whatever reason, we were off. She was lopping along at a good clip.

Now this was a new experience for me – as I said, I knew nothing about horses, let alone near blind and old horses.

I could not know that what we were setting about doing would be considered unheard of, but this beautiful old horse was going to prove in still another way what made her so special. This would be a long, hard run for any horse one way, not to mention a round trip.

I quickly got into the swing of things. Old Myrt was a good teacher, and I thrilled with a feeling that I now had the hang of it. As we passed our house, I must say that it looked strange from the back of a horse, but on and on we went until we came to a junction of the main road that had traffic on it going into Kennett. She was winded, and even I could see Myrt was not going to be able to make it any farther. I did not know what to do, but fortunately a family passing saw us could see that we were in distress and stopped.

I told them about our emergency, and I asked if they would go into town and get the doctor. I did not believe Myrt could go any longer. I asked him to please hurry out to the bridge that was only about an eighth of a mile this side of the Mitchell House. There he would find Morley in the water and several people there with him. He would be easy to find.

Turns out, they knew the family, and one of their kids knew the horse I was riding, and asked how I got Myrt to let me ride her. "You won't believe it, but I fed her some banana pudding," I replied.

They all laughed and the lady said, "I see you've hurt yourself." She meant my leg, but before I could explain, the man said they had better hurry and drove off.

Now I turned my attention to getting this old horse some much needed water. I nudged her over to the ditch alongside of the road where there was water. It was not fresh but it was suitable for drinking. She proceeded to do just that, and I made the mistake of getting off her as I had seen cowboys do in the movies.

I found it almost impossible to remount, not because she would not let me, but because my leg was so sore. It was hurting something awful. So there was not anything to do but try to drag my leg along. I tried leaning on Myrt while we walked on our way back from whence we had come. I was in such pain that I could not go any farther.

In a kind of desperation, I managed to lead Myrt over to a tree stump and was only just able to get on top of it. I fell over onto the back of the horse, again on the wrong side, but this time she allowed it. I think she sensed I was in great pain. It was all I could do to get sitting upright in the saddle. I was so thankful I could now turn everything over to her to get us home.

And she did.

Somewhere on the way back, I lost consciousness and fell forward over her neck. The next thing I was aware of was the clippety-clop sound her hooves made as we crossed the wooden bridge Morley had been catapulted from. There was no one in sight, so with a renewed vigor we broke into a lope and shortly were back. The doctor's Model-A Ford was there. He had taken a shortcut and beaten us back.

I tried to get off the horse and fell flat on my face. I must have yelled out because Dad was right there, seeing to me. First thing I asked about Morley, and was told that the doctor was sure that he was going to be all right. Mr. Mitchell and Dad had been able to get him up onto the bank, which took some doing because the bank was slippery and steep. They ran the risk of further hurting him by moving him, but it was felt necessary and they had carried him most of the way home when the doctor drove by.

Morley had had a very narrow escape. He had fallen some fifteen feet and had his fall broken by the water before he hit that tree trunk. He became caught on a limb, and that had kept his head above water. Everyone tried to appear positive and agreed that it could have been a lot worse. However, he would need to get several days of bed rest, and it would be necessary to keep him away from any excitement.

Old Doc said he wanted Mr. Mitchell to come in to see him. He wanted to discuss what he thought might have made Morley do something so dangerous like that. As he was leaving, he stopped and looked at me, kind of smiled, and said, "You must be the pudding boy. Say, you look hurt yourself! How'd that happen?"

He felt my brow and said, "The folks who told me I was needed here said there was a boy riding an old, blind horse that was known to be ill tempered. One that wouldn't let just anyone ride. Said he stopped them as they were returning from a visit with their folks, and asked them to get a doctor. One of their children knew this horse and his history of being temperamental, so they said, 'How did you get the old horse to let you ride?' and they said you told them you fed old Myrt some banana pudding." As he laughed he said, "Is that right?"

"Yessir," I said.

"Well I never heard of that before, but if it works that good then I wouldn't mind having some for myself," Old Doc laughed again.

"Where are my manners?" Mrs. Mitchell asked quickly, and set about serving him up some.

While she was at it, he asked if I minded him looking at my leg, and I told him no. Dad said he would be obliged if he would, so after some "uh hums," "I see now," and "how does this feel," he opened his black bag and took out some tubes of what turned out to be white, creamy, cool salve. He let me hold several of them.

Then he found a rather large bottle of something he called Ma-Crescent, along with some cotton, and he said, "This won't hurt much." But it did.

He proceeded to clean my wound all over again, and then dried it with more cotton. After that, he applied that cool, soothing cream all over the damaged part of my leg. He said to my dad that I had been through quite an ordeal myself, and I needed to be off my leg. He gave Dad a roll of bandages and said I would have to keep the wound clean and wrapped up.

"The things I gave you are all samples, so there will be no charge."

Dad and Mother both thanked him and he said, "No it's this young feller who should be thanked, for I can see he went through a lot just to make sure that I got here. Now I see he was hurt more than Morley was, even before he set off on that long ride. I'd say he's pretty brave."

Then he set about eating his banana pudding, and we just stood around with me thinking,

I wonder if he would go for it like that if he knew that I had fed it to Myrt straight from the bowl.

Oh well, guess it did not make no difference. He at least had gotten some, and me, who wanted some most of all, had not gotten any. It was not long after that when everything had been talked out, Morley put to bed, and the immediate danger had passed that it was decided that we should be leaving. The dinner was burned to such a condition that it had to be thrown away on account that the roast was forgotten about, as was the cornbread. What was going to be the mashed potatoes were scorched because they had all been left on the stove as everyone responded to this emergency by running after Morley. That led me to believe that this was not the first time he had gone off the deep end, so to speak.

Well that explains how we came to know the Mitchell family. As you can well see, it was a disaster. I still cannot understand how so many things could go so wrong in one short morning. But the Mitchell's, as it turned out, were not a family that took their disappointments as anything except something to be overcome.

And boy, did they ever. We did too, well, after our embarrassment had worn off, which was after about four weeks and I was mostly healed up. We learned that the last couple of years Mr. Denny Mitchell had been very busy. We all knew he had bought several hundred acres of what we believed to be worthless land. It was low and subject to flooding far more than would be expected, even for that part of the country. He bought it from two old squatters who had been on it since he himself had come here close to three years past.

Right about this time, some three years ago, as a matter of fact. His managers had instructed him to make the purchases. Had it been left up to him, that land would have been the last place in the world where he would have spent a nickel of his own money.

However, it was not Mr. Mitchell's money, and at that time, he was doing exactly what his handlers told him to do. They had put up the money, and he was told to build there, which he had done. He now realized the reason he was still alive was that he had been quick to carry out their instructions without questions.

Ch. 4: Gobler Is A Success.

Since our disastrous visit, Mr. Mitchell had bought two other horses from a fellow over in Tennessee who shod horses for a living. It was known that this fellow, Mr. Thurston Watson, knew horses, so Denny went to meet him and get a look at another horse that Mr. Watson had for sale.

Denny made a special trip over to Reelfoot Lake in Tennessee. After seeing the horse, he bought him and named him Fleet Foot from Reel Foot, Tennessee. While he was there, he also saw another horse that he liked the looks of and he bought him as well. This one, he would name Bob Tail, for obvious reasons. He thought about naming him Athlete's Foot, but afterwards he was glad he did not because Bob Tail would not budge onward from the starting line at the beginning of the first and only race he would ever run.

When the starting gun was fired, he neighed and whinnied, reared up, kicked out, and bucked around, nearly throwing his rider off so many times he plumb lost the reins. Then he leaped off the line. At this point, with the jockey barely managing to hold on, if it had not been for one very important thing, we thought he might be able to make up for lost time.

The only thing was he was running in the wrong direction. He proceeded to run right through the camping area where some of the campers had hung out clothes to dry on a makeshift line. The clothes were still wet, and he managed to take most of them with him. It was then that the rider got Mrs. Whittaker's knee-length, blue-and-white-striped bloomers wrapped around his head.

The poor jockey could not see a thing, and a low tree limb caught him and knocked him off. Nevertheless, he was a game lad and scampered to his feet, all the while fighting to get free of the bloomers. He was the last person to see Bob Tail high-tailing it away as he cleared a temporary wood-rail fence that surrounded the camping area. That jockey was so mad that he took off his gold and blue racing jacket, slung it to the ground, and jumped up and down on it, completely disgusted by the whole thing.

Then he set off after Bob Tail, who was still bucking as though he was trying to shed the saddle. The jockey finally left the fairgrounds, headed for parts unknown, only to return a short while later carrying his boots, but with no Bob Tail in tow. Later that night, however, some of the campers' washing was found floating in a quicksand bog. Everyone thought it was more than possible that was where Bob Tail ended up. Escaping that, he probably would have been killed by one of the many panthers known to inhabit the area.

When those clothes were found floating in the quicksand, the hunt for Bob Tail was called off. We did not actually take up the search for him until after dark that day, and really none of us was any too anxious to be going to begin with. As it was, we hunted with carbide lamps and were just to the point of turning back when someone yelled, "Be careful! We're at the quicksand!" Then he called out, "Look there!"

He had found what appeared to be some clothes still on a makeshift clothesline. We found a long tree limb, managed to retrieve the clothesline and – don't you know – while we were at it, we ourselves began to sink in over our shoes. It was dangerous work in that bog. We could not see where solid ground became mush. Several of us were able to extricate ourselves and decided it was time to get away from there.

We figured this was where Bob Tail bought the farm. That horse was beyond our help, but we thought it good that none of us joined him.

On the brighter side, we really did not know if Bob Tail had actually been swallowed up by that quicksand or not. Someone laughed and said it was possible that Bob Tail had been going so fast that when he found the sinkhole, he just skimmed across it before the quicksand could pull him down. He could be out there somewhere, without a scratch on him. If that were the case and the big cats didn't get him, he would just come on home on his own.

We had done all we could for the night, so we decided to turn homeward ourselves. We hoped that Bob Tail would not be startled by some damn fool like the one who fired that starting gun. You see, he was positioned on the outside, just where the official starter stood, as it were, close to Bob Tail's ear. It is sufficient to say that when he fired the starting pistol, Bob Tail was startled.

Startled? Why, I should say terrified. It is fair to say he would probably be running yet if he had not been bogged down in that quicksand.

That is the way it was the first time I saw them square off against a field of twelve. That beautiful reddish-brown stallion, Fleet Foot, ran out in front of the pack, with Morley as his jockey. Morley was just crazy enough to take all the dangerous chances necessary to win, which he did by at least twenty lengths.

This time, Mr. Denny Mitchell "cleaned up" –- that is to say, he raked in the money. It was the first fall race that year. It was part of our first County Fair, the year being 1942, which was held in a large clearing carved right out of the wilderness by Morley's enterprising father.

The warden of the Missouri State Penitentiary supplied convict labor to help, we would later learn, for certain monetary considerations, of course.

Those few who knew anything about it at the time thought it was free labor. We knew almost nothing about the possibility of getting convict labor to work the land. I suppose that was why this work was ultimately done on the QT.

Thinking about it, none of us really knew much about Denny Mitchell, except that when he moved to our County Line Road, he seemed to be, as was said back then, rather well-heeled. These convicts did lots of hard, dangerous work for Denny Mitchell several years back as well. He carved out a place for a settlement and named it "Gobler."

Before Denny Mitchell had built his large, corrugated monstrosity, what he called a warehouse, on what the locals – well, two old hermits who lived there anyway – said was right in the middle of the ancestral home for wild turkeys.

Why, what else could he name his new township but Gobler?

So it was that he pulled some strings to have the railroad bring a spur from the main line out of Deering down to his warehouse. He also carved out a three-mile racetrack, cutting right through the virgin forest; thirty or forty feet wide in places, which in itself was no small feat. It twisted around and cut through not only the pristine timber, but also split in half Southeast Missouri's largest sloughs and quicksand bogs.

That was no matter to him. The track continued around and finally cut across a good-sized stream before coming full circle. It went completely around the wilderness location, Gobler, Missouri.

Now, they did not bother to pull out all of the stumps on this crude racetrack, but they did manage to drag most of the fallen trees out of the way and line them along both sides of what was to be the racetrack.

There were lots of them, I might add; it was not neat, and it sure was not pretty. Still, it had to do; it was the only racetrack in the whole county. Well, maybe Saint Louis had one, I don't know for sure, but we sure had one: Gobler's very own regulation sized, three-mile long, give or take a hundred yards or so, racetrack.

Anyway, the excitement of all this just about guaranteed that Denny Mitchell's wholesale warehouse, racetrack and social emporium at Gobler would be an overnight success. And when he finally got it opened up, it was.

Mr. Denny, as everyone liked to call him, sold everything from soup to nuts there at Gobler. He bought most everything by the carload, railroad car that is. Since he advertised buying it by the car lot, he got it cheaper and he sold it cheaper.

He sold things like nick-knacks, do-dads, and fiddle-frattle, as well as bricker-bracks and what-nots. He sold them all for cash, naturally.

When it came to big-ticket items, however, like farm equipment and household goods, well, for those things he advertised that sometimes "suitable arrangements could be worked out." He meant payment terms, of course, but no one in that part of the country would ever be so bold as to talk about credit, so Mr. Denny did not call it that. That is just what it was, but to be able to buy things on time, as it was so delicately put, well it was just necessary to agree to some steep terms. Some said they were steep anyway, but his prices were more reasonable than the company store.

Mr. Denny was very good at math, and he could figure

in his head faster than any of us farmers could with a pencil and pad. He told us that he would sell cheaper to us, anything we bought, than we would pay anywhere else. By anywhere else, he meant the Great General American Land Company Store. He was good to his word, and it helped that Mr. Denny and his family were nice people.

That initial unpleasantness we all experienced was not to cloud our further relations with them, either personal-wise or business-wise.

They were very friendly, neighborly, as a matter of fact. They were liked by almost everyone. That's the reason we all believed that people came from far away, enduring the most unfavorable situations, just to get to Gobler.

Coming into Gobler, you left the main road, the hard surface road, and started heading through the timber. From there on, you only had one way in or out, and it was only a cut made right alongside the spur, just wide enough for one vehicle, be it wagon, truck, or car – or tractor as was often the case, to either come or go.

Naturally, the trouble really began when you met someone going as you were coming, or coming as you were going. Someone had to give way and that in and of itself was not really a problem. For the most part, we were always ready to accommodate one another. The real difficulty came if it had been raining or was starting to rain. If the road, such as it was, was real wet and slippery, the whole thing turned into one long mud hole and it became necessary to push, pull, lift, pry or anything else we could do. That included trying to build up under the tires and wheels anything solid, usually limbs and saplings that we could find.

All of this was usually for naught, because we were dealing with world-class gumbo, and I don't mean the kind you can eat. You can imagine the thrill we would get when we finally got free of the mud. Then, of course, the disappointment that would follow when we would get stuck again.

Going to Mr. Denny's was, for the women and girls at least, an occasion for dressing up, so it was especially upsetting when they would get stuck. The men folk would insist that the ladies and young ones stay out of the mud and one or more would strike out on foot to Mr. Denny's at Gobler where, for just such emergencies – which were not uncommon – he kept a small but very old Caterpillar with a large grader blade on the front.

While we waited, we used the time to get to know one another.

I did say that people came from a long way off to get to Mr. Denny's. Since we were all stuck there, we put in the time visiting and getting to each other, until finally we would hear the sound of that little Cat coming to push or pull us out of the mud.

That was not a small job. Sometimes as many as six or eight vehicles would be backed up going into Gobler, and sometimes just as many going out. The little Cat never failed in its task, untangling that mess and sending us on our way. Everyone was good-natured and friendly about it all, and the most important thing was that nothing broke down, and the women and girls did not get their Calicos, pretty crinolines and their starched and freshly ironed flowery dresses muddy. If the ladies' slippers and Sunday frocks were not maimed, then all was not lost when we finally reached Mr. Denny's.

The farming folks could spend some pleasant time seeing what was new – all the nick-knacks, patty-whacks, lotions, potions and notions that Mr. Denny had to choose from.

Mr. Denny had a rather large generator sitting outside that provided electricity so he was able to have electric lights. He also had two huge floor fans that put out a lot of wind. Naturally, the young started making a game of it by walking or running in front of the fans.

One could not help but notice how it managed to blow the older girls' skirts up. While they made a fuss, they would usually come back to see if it would do it again. The mothers would pretend to scold and look to see if anyone had noticed. We boys always did, even at my young age of ten. I suspected that the girls rather liked it, and I know with a certainty the boys did.

Ch. 5: Singing Cowboys Entertain Us

Everyone appreciated the lights and the wind, especially in the summer. As if these wonders were not enough for us to marvel over, there was more. For our enjoyment, Mr. Denny placed a large floor model, light brown wooden Motorola radio in his department store. He had it set right over by the phonograph records and sheet music. It had a big black battery hidden behind it. From this beautiful radio, we heard Eddie Arnold sing his Cattle Call song. Bob Nolen and the Sons of the Pioneers would sing Cool, Cool Water.

The Sons of the Pioneers included a man by the name of Leonard Sly, but the world would later know and love him as Roy Rogers. We would sometimes get to listen to Bob Wills and his Light Crust Dough Boys, coming to us courtesy of Pappy O'Daniels from as far away as Fort Worth, Texas. We heard Bob McKnight, who we all knew was blind, singing Old Shep, and there would not be a dry eye in the place. It was like a religious experience.

I suppose it was, especially the part about if dogs have a Heaven, then Old Shep would have a wonderful home. We could also hear the Old Camp Meeting Time program, which featured several groups that were all family members singing Gospel songs. We heard the Stamps Baxter Quartet, the Carter Family Camp Fire Singers, and The Old Round-Up Gang. There were others too, like early Red Foley, a very young Margaret Whiting, Jimmy Wakeley, "…and many others," as the radio announcer always said.

It may interest you to know, these guys we called "the Singing Cowboys" weren't really cowboys as in guys herding cattle about but we didn't know that then. They were more likely singers that got wind of how much us in the hinterlands of the country loved anything that had to do with cowboys, especially songs sung out on a prairie by one lone cowboy (maybe he had a "chorus" of other cowboys that just happened to chime in on the refrain - and what was that we'd hear? Anywhere from one guitar to a complete orchestra that magically appeared out there amongst the steers just when the singing cowboy needed it – why, we didn't care – it all seemed right to us). Or maybe a quartet of singing cowboys who didn't need anything to accompany them except themselves, and of course it just so happened that each voice part (you know, the real high, the medium high, the medium low, the real low) was represented by those four voices.

Them old boys generally wore big white cowboy hats, representing as they did the good ole boy with a heart of gold in the body of a cowboy, just what this country needed to prove to itself it was the best, the most honest of all countries, which I did and do believe it was and is. I don't reckon the "cowboy" period in this country lasted but a few years, but we all took that period to heart, putting forth as it did the cowboy as the pure-T example of the best the country had to offer – quiet American heroes that used their true grit to overcome the hardships of the trail. And it wasn't all made up neither.

Not many years before them singing cowboys was crooning to us, the real-life cowboys were out there on those plains driving cattle across the country, and sure enough singing to each other at the end of each long, weary day. As difficult as it was, that hardscrabble life under the open sky was something most of us knew wouldn't last much longer, with the country filling up with such things as settlers and electricity.
Wish I had been there myself, but you don't get to pick your time now, do you?
Back then, there was everybody from Gene Autry, Tex Ritter and Roy Rogers, amongst whole groups of lesser knowns.

Looking back on those times, music was just a big part of everything, and not just the Singing Cowboys either.

Radios were everywhere, and the choice of what to listen to ran from folks like Woodie Guthrie, singin' about the heartland of our country – to little 16-year-old Doris Day singing with Les Brown's band – to Bing Crosby — to the big bands. Now them big bands was something – it's hard to say why they caught on as big as they did exactly when they did, but I think it had something to do with the terrible war in Europe (and almost over here). There was just something special about the sound; it was a pick-me-up when we Americans, why, people all over the world, especially needed one.

Come in on a late Friday night after working in the fields a good solid week and then some, get yourself a plate of cornbread and a glass of buttermilk, set yourself down and as the song said, "Turn Your Radio On, Listen to the Music in the Air" – maybe the great Glenn Miller holding forth with "In the Mood." There almost nothing better. Then would come Tommy Dorsey and "I'll Never Smile Again," reminding everyone that our troops were overseas and their loved ones were back at home anxiously waiting for their return.

And speaking of Tommy Dorsey, how 'bout that nifty young Frank Sinatra he brought in to sing with the band. Have to admit I thought he was the greatest, and I never lost that liking for Mr. Sinatra as long as I lived.

Oh, then there were the ladies: Kate Smith with that big, brash voice that could tame any big band, and, oh boy, those cutesy-shabootsey Andrews Sisters, singin' that tight harmony that was the way to every man's heart! There was even some of that high-falootin' what they call classical music every once in a while on the radio – like symphonies and such.

Now Mr. Denny, he was one who kept his finger on the likes and dislikes of those of us who bought his stuff, so don't you know he had a whole set of shelves filled with published sheet music for sale. Mostly he had single popular songs done up in a piano arrangement, maybe with some guitar chords, so anybody who had a piano or guitar could at least pick out the notes underneath the singer. Oh, he had "Bewitched, Bothered and Bewildered" by Hart and Rodgers, "The Breeze and I," "Fools Rush In," "I Hear Music" – all the most popular pieces. Well, and a few other pieces that the fellers would laugh over since it seemed there might be more than one meaning behind the words, if you get my drift: Fats Waller's "All That Meat and No Potatoes." And a few sung by that beautiful sad lady Billie Holiday – "God Bless the Child" and others. Music wise, well, it seemed we had everything a heart could desire and much more, no matter if we might have been a mite poor in other ways.

Oh, we were royally entertained. Without a doubt, these programs featured the best of the best singers who ever lived. Well, we thought so anyway.

 It could have been that just at Gobler, way out in that forested area, the added delight of this great music coming to us from almost every part of that huge, corrugated building was what really made it special. He had placed the speakers up about twenty feet apart all around the place to really spread out the sound.

Mr. Denny had also provided us with an ice cream parlor serving cordials, with plenty of scrolled, painted chairs to sit in so we could rest our feet. This was especially important for the women in their dress shoes.

He also kept the place cool. He placed cotton up underneath the ceiling and fixed it there with wire mesh. It served as insulation against the heat and sun and made the building warm in the winter. I do believe I mentioned that Mr. Denny was a smart man, and that right there is the proof. We did not think anyone had thought of anything like that before. It made the place comfortable and so we could browse, see or be seen, catch up on the latest gossip and maybe reflect upon the weightier decisions to be made about the weather or making a large-ticket purchase.

Looking back on it, I really do believe that by setting aside that comfortable area, which just happened to look out on the main traffic as it came by – meaning looking out on people, of course – though it may not have been intended as such, it became a place where you could sit and wait with dignity.

It was even the case if you had to remove your shoes for your feet being sore. It was a place you could wait for your muse to return and maybe enjoy a nickel dish of ice cream.

Mr. Denny kept the ice cream stored in dry ice. We did not even know there was such a thing. He had five flavors for us to enjoy. Vanilla, chocolate, and strawberry – he claimed the strawberries inside were fresh picked and we never questioned it – were the three staples. In addition to that, he had two new flavors, what he called Tutti-Frutti, which was green with a taste like mint and wintergreen with little bits of what looked like marshmallows; and Pistachio, which was a lighter green and had several kinds of nuts and candied cherries.

For only a nickel you could get a double scoop of either one, or mix them up if you wanted.

Imagine buying that for a nickel now! Of course, back then, it was hard to come by a nickel if you were a kid.

Still, it was pleasant just to sit and enjoy an ice cream cordial, kick off your shoes as so many would do, and relax. I know that this pleasantness of mind translated into many large-ticket purchases that otherwise would not have been made.

Looking back, I picked up on this as a sign of genius on the part of Mr. Denny Mitchell – we all thought he had seen a vision – and if he was not an out-and-out genius, he was for sure a man ahead of his time.

We just knew he had been given a revelation in which he saw things none of the rest of us could see, and what's more, he acted on it. I for one believed he truly loved what he accomplished. It was all people talked about: "Let's go see what's going on down at Denny's!"

Now while he may not have actually cared about the success of this place at first, we all really believed he was a dedicated man pursuing a dream. He acted on a vision that showed him how things could be down there in the swamp. At least, he sure acted like he did, yes sir, and he acted on it, as we were wont to say.

True, that was said, but other things were said as well, and I fear if the truth be known, the local men who he hired to do the work of clearing away, building up and hauling off timber limbs often made sport of him, behind his back, of course.

I know for a certainty that some of the very men who needed the work most, all of them in fact, called the undertaking Denny's Folly, and others referred to it as

Mitchell's Madness.

Be that as it may, the work went on, and finally where nothing but wilderness had been before, though fortified as it were by such an undergrowth of briars, thorns and vines so much so that neither man nor beast could pass.

Well, except for the two old hermits who owned the wilderness and lived on the higher ground in a lean-to. Everyone thought of them as crazy. They had to be to live where they lived. Other than these two old recluses, no one wanted to go there. Maybe one might go for a short visit. If a man went there willingly, which was rarely the case, he certainly would not want to be caught there after dark.

It just would not be the best policy. The vastness and thickness of it made the place all the more formidable. Add to this mix a forest of ancient cypress sporting some of the tallest knees the men who worked the timber had ever seen – four to four and a half feet tall, though mostly confined to the swamp. On the higher ground were the hickory, sweet gum, black oak and walnut trees.

Animals there could feed off pecans, berries, crawdads and persimmon. The entire area was a paradise for wildlife.

The one time that I was in the swamp, before it had been improved upon, I counted six coon dens in the cypress trees alone. What a feast they must have had, too. There were crayfish mounds – we boys called them castles –

everywhere I looked.

We called those crayfish mudbugs and crawdads, and they, like the berries, were without number. Black berries, purple berries, red berries, all sorts grew there. One could not walk without crunching pecans and hickory nuts under foot.

All that bounty was there for the taking, but sad to say, it was the exact place Mr. Denny decided to build. So, in the middle of all of that was this almost unbelievable accomplishment. Now this strange looking, large corrugated steel building dominated the place. A single railroad track ended beside a sturdy loading platform built exactly in the center of the long structure with a large receiving door, so that it was only necessary for the train cars to be switched on the spur. This was done about a mile or so away, and then they would coast right in front of the loading dock. It only required one brakeman to handle, it was simple and neat, and all of us farmers could only marvel.

We were not alone in this, for people came from as far away as Cape Girardeau, Poplar Bluff, New Madrid and Sikestou. When he finally got the place open, Mr. Denny found that the number of people who came far exceeded the space he had laid out as a parking area. As a result, people just parked in the edge of the forest close by, which they could easily do if it was not wet or raining. Some of the places they came from were sixty or seventy miles away. To make such a trip was no small undertaking even on a good road. Doing it in one day was risky.

Still, people came, even when gas and just about everything else was rationed. Even with coupons, good gas was as much as twenty cents a gallon in some places. Word got out, though, that a new place called Gobler was built out in the middle of nowhere. The only road was rough, and when it rained it was near impossible. It was not on any map at the time, but Mr. Denny had a slogan: "If you got to have it, and I ain't got it, then I will get it".

It was a bold declaration by a man who named a town site in honor of wild turkeys. It brought people into Gobler. They wanted to meet the man who thought so much of turkeys, and when they came they were pleasantly surprised by all they saw. So it became a place easy to remember, if not easy to get to, which really only added to its mystique. Mr. Mitchell himself remained a well cultivated mystery and yes, even a man of intrigue.

How was he able to get all those things that were hard, if not impossible, for anyone else to get?

A war was going on, and it did not take long for word to travel that he, as he so tactfully put it, could get those things most hard to come by. Some things he already had, and certain large-ticket items he could get in about two weeks. It did not matter if it was tires, a car, tractor, radio batteries or rubber boots. He sold sugar by the twenty-pound bag. He kept dried prunes and apricots, sold canned Alberta peaches and sweet Northern pears in ten-sized cans. He sold those only by the case of twenty-four. He had twenty-five and fifty pound bags of self-rising flour and slops for pigs, all with pretty flowers and other designs that sold pretty well.

The women wanted their husbands to buy the flour with the pretty pictures on the sacks. They made dresses and shirts out of them. Women knew how to sew their own clothes then, provided they had the material for it. That was why they wanted those sacks, and believe me they made some mighty pretty things out of them.

Our women and girls kept themselves in beautiful skirts and blouses. Some had acorns on them, some had oak leaves. Some had tiny little animals, and some just had a simple design in several different colors. When the big lots of flour had been sold and the flour used, it wasn't unusual to see, of an evening, several women and girls gathered out on a front porch with the freshly washed flour sacks, comparing fabric designs and deciding what to swap for what.

And don't you know when those dresses and shirts began to wear out, here came the grandmothers to take them apart, cut them up, combine several patterns and colors together and make the prettiest quilts you ever saw. Oh, they were simple – just squares of different colored cloth sewed together for a top, then a layer of soft batting in the middle and a plain muslin backing, sewed through so they wouldn't slip and then threaded here and there with little ties of brightly colored yarn just for the look of it.

One of the things I loved the most about the way we

lived back then was our attempt not to waste one thing, to use up even the scraps of food and cloth we had left over for another, newer purpose – so when we were finished, we were really finished.

Food leftovers or extras got preserved in some fashion. We pickled cucumbers and made sauerkraut from fresh cabbage. We had a root cellar that stayed tolerably cool most times but would not freeze the turnips and beets and potatoes we stored down there through the winter, although we occasionally lost some vegetables or fruits to various marauding animals, especially those pesky and hilarious raccoons whose delicate little hands were so clever they could have performed surgery, had the coons had a mind to.

And wives and daughters busied themselves pretty near every day making fresh biscuits or bread or noodles for chicken soup or crust for the blackberry cobbler out of the flour in those pretty sacks. Then sometimes the boys would get a shirt made from those sacks (if there was enough left over after the ladies made their lovely dresses), which to us was the latest in fashion.

Mr. Denny also stocked some barbed wire and nails of various sizes. He had leather goods, shoes, harnesses and the like. When it came to such things as cultivators, disks, harrows and so forth, not to mention furniture like tables and chairs for the house, all he kept was floor samples of those things for you to order. He also had several large radios on the floor for sale, much as he had for us to listen to when we visited. I know he sold quite a few of them to us country folk.

To get back to those large-ticket purchases, if he did not have it, if something else would not do, well he only needed a few days. Quite naturally, he would need money down, which we all readily agreed was only right. Mr. Denny sure seemed alright with us. Take, for instance, the times that he would send ration coupons to one or another of us so we could buy whatever it was we were a little short on money to buy. He did this for twenty-four cents on the dollar.

We knew everything was rationed and required coupons, so when he would do this for one of us, we understood this was a very special thing. We began to buy everything we needed from Mr. Denny, especially things that were overpriced at the Company Store. Many of us would never have had nice things if it were not for Denny Mitchell. We never really knew how he was able to do things like that, and we never asked questions neither.

Looking back now, it is easy to see that we were not a very bright bunch. But we were not stupid either. We knew the who, what, when, where and sometimes why of things, especially when we suspected that something shady might be going on.

As it referred to Mr. Denny, we knew we did not need to know, so we did not ask.

It was obvious that in all other respects, what was going on back then was big news. Mr. Denny was venturing forth in the truest pioneering spirit. We all sincerely believed, and this sounds like a poor pun, that he was blazing a new trail, albeit not a very good one as it looked on the surface of things. A trail he blazed just the same, and I have often thought what a shame that none of this was really on the up and up.

But more about that later.

Now those who might consider the irreparable damage that his trail blazing caused to the ecology should know the damage caused by that initial assault on this primordial setting quickly repaired itself. In truth, some scars remained, which was to be expected. Most troubling was the manner in which the many large trees were removed to open up that part of the swamp and create what barely passed for a racetrack. It was a steeplechase, an endurance run and one hell of an obstacle course all rolled into one. For reasons none of us could really understand, it was also to be Denny Mitchell's pride and his showcase. More so, I am afraid, than his huge wholesale warehouse, which turned out from the start to be successful.

The track, as he would proudly refer to it, would turn out to be – well I should be careful here. I do not want to get too far ahead of myself. I have a lot of ground to cover before the why of everything falls into place.

That racetrack played an important part in everything that was to come. So please bear with me a little longer, and I will do my best to make this as interesting as possible for you. When we finally realized what was really going on around us, we found it almost impossible to believe. I still do now.

Ch. 6: Convicts Perish In The Swamp

It was not very hard to decide that one of the things that needed to be done was to improve that long, bug-hued dirt road that we had to tackle coming into and leaving Gobler. At first, it was a novelty. People looked at negotiating that road as a challenge – one taken reluctantly – and it was not long before that challenge offered bragging rights for those who made it.

Over time, though, the crowd tired of the challenge, and people wanted to know when Mr. Denny was going to do something about his road. Some even made it sound like a threat, "Guess you gonna pay to have new bearings put on the front axle of my old Chevy, huh Mr. Denny?"

And so on and so on, until there was no longer any doubt that people were tired of having to deal with it. By now, it was beginning to seem like a real inconvenience. To tell the truth, it had *always* been a real inconvenience, but it was the only so-called "road" into the Gobler complex. Since the newness had worn off, some said if Mr. Denny called that a road, then they might call his other creations a stigma, or a dilemma – a work of the primitive, a blight, an eyesore!

Which if it had not been built where it was is exactly what it would have been, an eyesore. You would never expect to see such a complex built down in the deep swamp. Your first thought was that this could not be, but it was; and it was to catch hold and prove to be just what the people wanted.

Except, of course, for that road, which Mr. Denny was reluctantly going to do something about, eventually. By now you might have come to realize he was a juggler of the first rank. Otherwise, he could not have kept so many things going at once. As it turned out, more than a few of his dealings were shady – but at that time, we did not know the half of it.

Now if I did not already bring this up, it is time I did, for slowly but surely the pressure became such that he was becoming a nervous wreck. He was by now chain smoking and had started drinking quite a bit.

His misgivings about some of his business dealings were beginning to affect his health. Not only had he used convict labor, but also during that time, two prisoners had been killed. He knew they were killed for no justifiable reason and since then he had not been able to shake the feeling that in some way it was his fault.

These two men were killed during the initial and hardest part of the work, the first cut-through of that terrible slough. There were snakes in there, the largest known and the likes of which I do not believe had ever been identified. Spiders of every kind, big and bigger, lived in that place. It was the ancestral home not only of wild hogs but of deer of every kind known to North America – well we thought so anyway – and every carnivore known to pray on them. That included black panthers and even bears, sure signs of which surfaced when work began on the clearing. And there were even packs of feral dogs, offspring, no doubt, of family dogs which had gotten themselves either lost or left behind when a family moved or a patriarch died.

In that deep wood, we had bats and birds of most every kind, owl, hawks, doves and even some eagles from time to time. Yes, as far as was determined we had every kind of North American bird but pheasant.

Nope, no pheasants were to be found there. Although we had some real strange birds known as "peasants". Lots of us in town, why we were ourselves rather pleasant peasants, you might say. But alas, we had no pheasant.

There were frogs – that swamp was nothing less than a nursery of every kind and color, the likes of which had rarely been seen outside of our slough. Now not only were they there in all those different colors, but some of them could easily jump ten feet or more. Some said they had tongues that were more than twice as long as their own bodies.

Before we realized just how unusual they really were, we had gigged a passel of 'em, I am sad to say. Their legs were good to eat if they were fried up like chicken.

Last but certainly not least, we had insects of every description. Now before I go any farther I want to tell you about another peculiarity: our fireflies. We had them without number. About the only thing we had more of in the summer and early fall down there in that deep swamp was mosquitoes, and we had both by the millions.

According to our local gentry – I never saw this for myself. This story was told to me by those men, and I figure it came from a good source. But I will let you be the judge.

Our local gentry had a story about the peculiar nature of man, of our frogs, and the effect our fireflies had on them down in the swamp. It was said that those frogs would just crawl upon a big lily pad, there were thousands of them in the swamp, and just after dark, those fireflies would converge over the water just a-winkin' and a-blinkin'. Some said they were coming out that way to make a sign to whatever other firefly they had taken a shine to.

As the fireflies were doing their dance of life, what really was a dance of death for them, our frogs sitting there on those lily pads would wait until they could get them lined up six or eight across and then zap that long tongue and reel in at least a half dozen or more at a time.

They would thus fill up on those glow worms so fast that it would light them up from inside. Because of the great quantity that those frogs ate, the additional weight taken on would cause the frogs to gradually sink. The frogs would sit there on the bottom winking on and off.

If the frog was blue then he would give off a blue glow. If red then he would give off a red glow, if green – as most of them were – then they would just blink on and off with a warm green glow. With the neon red and the dusty blue colors emanating from those frogs sitting there on the bottom, that swamp was turned into a sea of ever changing green, blue, and red, warm patterns of pulsating phosphorescent light.

Above were the brighter colors of the frogs on the lily pads, who as of yet had not sunk. Thousands more fireflies dallied around in that dank night air blinkin', winkin' and swoopin'. They would fly up and disappear, going dark. The swamp was full of frogs all in good voice. It would seem each joined in, ever louder, serenading each other. That place was alive with the sounds and sights of nature at its best and was in such complete harmony, fine-tuned such that every buzz, every croak, and every sound of the dark was just where it should be, just what it should be.

This place belonged to the night and all the animals haired, feathered, or otherwise belonged to it as well. This was their Lincoln Center for the Performing Arts, and it was not meant for mere humans to intrude. Because we did, we caused a great disharmony and broke their delicate balance and the working arrangement they had worked out with the Creator of it all. If this story be told because of this transgression against these creatures, if their Creator would forevermore deny the human being the right to see all of nature as it was in there nightly, I can only conclude that we are the poorer for it.

I was told that this was the way it was, long, long ago. They say that if you approach the edge of any wood or slough, even today, and are very, very quiet – if you listen close to the night breeze – if you stand perfectly still and watch the clouds play hide and peek with the yellow moon – if you just appreciate the wonder that surrounds you; you may never hear anything other than the soft evening breeze. However, you may hear other sounds, if you listen close.

Listen to the night bird calling, "Come here, Lenore. Here, Lenore. Here, Lenore. A raven answers never again, for I have sworn." Hear the barn owl swooping by, almost without a sound, a cricket sounding off somewhere out of sight, or a lone wolf howling. Listen to a red fox prowling or cicada drumming for a mate with all its might. If you do hear these things then you are truly a lucky one, for few people today get a chance to or can hear the music that awaits you in the night. I myself never had the opportunity to see this with the frogs and the fireflies, but it would have been something if it had really happened.

I do not see why it would not be true.

At that time, malaria was still prevalent, as well as yellow fever. Back then, we called all mosquito-borne illnesses the sweats, the shakes, or some such. We just knew it was bad, and all these dreaded things were there waiting in the swamp. Those convicts took it all, bent on facing terror with only an ax and saw.

All this work had been undertaken in the summer, usually without a shirt and sometimes no shoes by these poor souls who were apparently without any rights. They were not paid for their labor, and they worked under the mean sharp eyes of cold-blooded guards who, in contrast to the prisoners, wore fine expensive uniforms, black shiny boots, and official stylish hats. They rode beautiful, healthy looking horses with brown handmade saddles.

These guards carried some of the latest rifles, and would sit on their fine steeds and watch those poor dregs of society with murderous intent in their eyes. They carried full canteens with burlap wrap to keep the water cool, and when they would drink they would swish the first mouth full around in their mouth and for the effect it would have on those thirsty convicts. They would then spit it out, wasting even more as before. They would take a drink to swallow and then they would pour more out on the ground while the poor suffering out there working would have to beg for a short sip of water.

As often as not, if it was not asked for with just the right tone of respect towards a guard, they would be told, "It ain't water time yet. I'll tell you when you're thirsty. For now, all you've got to think about is how much more work you're gonna have to do for me before I call quittin' time. You understand me, boy?"

These men knew they were never far away from death, death from some unknown terror of the swamp or at the hands of the sadistic guards. These guards, for all it seemed, were just waiting for those convicts to break any one of a myriad of rules either written or otherwise. By their attitude, it would just make their day if they had the opportunity to shoot one of these miserable expendables. These guards looked at the convicts as being less than human anyway.

As for the need to justify such a killing, no such was required. That was the case with the two who were shot when they first took on that terrible encounter. The word of the guards was always that he was jumped by the prisoner he shot, or the prisoner was attempting to run. Rarely was a guard's word questioned. It really was just state-sanctioned murder by a bunch of thugs dressed up in fancy uniforms, no more and no less.

We country folks learned early in life if it walks like a skunk, looks like a skunk and smells like a skunk, then there is a better than average chance that it is a skunk.

It did not matter that their acts were given the appearance of respectability by those who called themselves law enforcement agents. They and we all knew it amounted to nothing less than plain murder every time they killed one of those prisoners. They sometimes did it for no justifiable reason; the guards were just mean and sadistic. They were hired by the state as guards "over these less fortunate." For that very reason, they could and did claim the shooting was necessary, and as it has been pointed out their word was almost never challenged.

In those perilous times, it did not matter if a man lived or died. It made little or no difference, for out on a chain gang, as they were almost always chained together, they would just unlock him after making sure he was dead, or too badly wounded to have to worry about, and have one or more of the other prisoners drag him aside.

Sometimes they laid him on a pile of brush where they could keep an eye on him, and he would stay there until the day's work was done. Then they would load those convicts back on what looked like six-by-six army trucks, and lead those beautiful horses back into their custom-designed trailers.

If it became necessary to shoot one of these prisoners, then that man, dead or alive, would be laid between the other prisoners' feet as they sat on benches on both sides of the rear of those trucks. As often as not in these situations, by the time all hands arrived back at the prison, if the man had only been wounded and somehow managed to stay alive until they left, he would usually be dead by the time they got back. If by some miracle he was still alive, then and only then would he receive medical attention.

For we weren't rightly a nation of law so much then as later, inasmuch as lots of locales in this country still had the look and feel of wilderness. Oh, there were laws on the books, but when you had to wait for the circuit-ridin' judge to come into the county from who knows what distance before you might get a case settled up proper, you see how that might lead to people takin' matters into their own hands. So if, every now and again, a feller known to be a "slick character," as they say, someone prone to taking advantage of unsuspecting settlers, just up and disappeared, why, it wasn't that unusual for a person like that, wouldn't you say? I'm not saying it was right. I'm just saying it happened.

Ch. 7: Saints Infiltrate The Community

Now I know that prisoner business is tough to hear, but it has everything to do with the saga of the Mitchell family. That poor crew of captive labor had been forced to shoulder the brunt of the hard and dangerous work that had to be done before any building could take place. Denny Mitchell had gotten in bed, so to speak, with some high-placed, crooked state officials and so-called businessmen in order to procure the services of the prisoners. In reality, those businessmen were the money bags behind a very large international "religious organization" whose desire for expanding their influence amounted to nothing less than fanaticism demanding success at any cost. If none of this had happened, then in all probability Mr. Denny would never have found himself in this terrible dilemma.

However, this evil group was laying the groundwork, leaving no stone unturned, doing all that was necessary to advance their hidden agenda. Alas, there was already a crack in their bell, a chink in their armor so to speak, and things were about to turn vicious. At this point, though, they were still putting forth the idea that whatever it took to accomplish God's work was justified.

Now where have we heard that before?

So, here we have these different players in Mr. Denny's fate: some were good, some bad, some simply indifferent – that is to say out-and-out ugly and in some cases just plain stupid and dumb. Then there were those who were plumb eaten up with greed, and others who were suffering from blind ambition.

But the worst of the lot were the so-called pillars of the church community. Their intent proved the most unforgiveable of the lot. For someone who was not caught up in their carryings on, it was possible to see that here were men and women of the church who had lost their way. They had sold out all their honorable principles in exchange for some political power that imagined would be bestowed on their organization by the new world masters, assuming, of course, that the Nazis won the war.

The stakes were so high that the church higher-ups had somehow managed to convince themselves that they had received a direct order from God to spread their particular doctrine. God, in fact, had singled them out to accomplish this by any means necessary, even up to and including selling out to fascism.

As they later stated, this bowing to the devil was a necessary, but only temporary, measure, until theirs could be made the official religion of North America, Canada and Mexico.

It would be possible only if Hitler were victorious, and they were certain he would be – *if* America did not come into the war on the side of Hitler's enemies, France and England.

Their stated purpose as far as we all knew was the

saving of souls by adding to their congregations all who were outside of God's embrace, meaning anyone who was not already a member of their faith. Whoever saved one of these lost souls, by whatever means necessary, was sure to curry God's favor instantly.

This group of zealots had worked out a master plan, to their own satisfaction anyway. And how to bring new converts into the fold by the hundreds?

(And I say what it amounted to was by hook or by crook...)

Their saying was, whatever it took.

One of their tried and proven methods was having the deacons make each member accountable for bringing a given number of new members in each month. Thus, when a member reached a certain level within the church, decided by a tally of newly saved souls he had brought in, he was singled out for high recognition and given membership in a special branch of the church. These upright citizens were thought to be only a little lower than the angels.

Well, I do not know about that, but it is true that they certainly began enjoying a much higher status within the church.

What's more, to help them become more readily recognizable, the church body furnished special robes of purple and white that they were required to wear while going about church business. They were also afforded the status of Saints, if you can believe that.

Those enjoying this special rank could select certain prospects, people who were not yet members. In order to encourage them to join, these members were authorized to make them a financial offer that it was felt no one could refuse. It did not take long before, as a matter of necessity, those offers were being made to all of us.

When all these new people began showing up in our locale, many of our local gentry wanted to know who they were. For the most part, it seemed that we just looked up one day to find them there among us. Right off, they had their church up and running. It seemed as though they became entrenched in our community almost before we knew what was going on. Of course, we had no idea that the ones making up this first wave were only the vanguard for stranger people to come. We noticed however, that they all seemed capable of handling several different tasks at a time.

For example, they began to put up brand-new houses, what they called "prefabs," and they could and did put them up quickly. First, big trucks came down our dirt road and spread gravel, making it an all-weather road. They said it was their gift to our county, and we could not deny that our old road needed the gravel. The county should have graveled it, but the county officials said that County Line Road was not the responsibility of Dunklin County, and we ought to be glad we were getting it graveled by these good folks.

In other words, the county was not asking any questions

about it, so why should we?

Next came these other large trucks carrying the prefabbed houses, built-in sections, frames and all. The only thing necessary was for four men or in this case, women and men to take them off these trucks and put them together. They had everything numbered and a plan to follow. These people knew what they were doing and they went immediately about it, wasting no time with no long breaks and extended lunches. And they could make fast work of it too; in fact, ten people could put as many as three four-roomed prefabricated houses together in one day – just get started early and work late.

All these quick changes taking place on our County Line Road was big news. We would go down after we left the field for the day and just stand around and watch the goings on until it got dark. They would still be putting the prefabs together, and the only sound would be the continuous sound of their hammers. Since everything was all cut to fit, no saws were necessary.

Ch. 8: Roads And Houses Go In

Now for us watching this activity was kind of like watching carnies put up a carnival. When the old carnival trucks would come down our road, we would be excited, but we always knew they would be leaving in a few days. But these people had obviously come to stay, although we did not fully realize it yet. They were well organized to include not only the putting together of these neat though ticky-tacky looking houses, but also the preparation of them. They also saw to the sending of meals to everyone and the all-important clean up after. Everything had to be left spic and span, and their attention to detail was something that did not go unnoticed, even as we watched from the ditch on our side of the newly graveled road.

When it came to cleanness and sanitation, it seemed they had a fetish. Looking back, "fetish" seems like just the right word because they looked as if they were driven by something more than just the work at hand. Many years later, I would see that same intensity enforced by the sergeant in charge of the mess halls, especially the KPs.

Of course, I was not yet part of the KPs, so when I first saw this, I did not know what name to put to it. What it really was, though, was a show of military discipline.

Of course, we just thought they were all business, and in that way, they seemed a little strange to us. Even though we were hardworking country folk, we had lots of simple joys and happiness in our everyday lives. We smiled with one another and told jokes. It was easy to see that though our lives were hard, we as a people were happy.

We were pleasant peasants, as I liked to say.

In contrast, these newcomers showed a certain austerity, coupled with nervous anxiety, especially by the women and girls. It was as though they were forever anticipating a command. In fact, one could not help but notice the undercurrent of unbridled authority on behalf of the men. It reminded me of the sort of German military discipline portrayed in the old movies at the tent shows.

This should have been a giveaway as to what these aloof, rigidly disciplined people – come, as they said, to "establish a New Zion" – were really about.

I remember thinking even then that I expected at any moment for one of them to snap to with a "Heil Hitler!" salute. I did not speak of it, just kept it to myself.

The women and girls were something to see! They had freshly scrubbed skin and glowing faces. Their hair was so clean it glistened, and they wore it up in a bun on the backs of their heads. As a group, they looked so healthy they scared me although we all noticed they were completely subordinate to the men. It seemed that what the men thought, the women thought, and they went about their duties without complaint, obedient and quick to carry out every order given to them. They never seemed to tire, never lolly-gagged (even when there was nothing urgent to do) and always stayed busy, displaying that nervous demeanor as they scurried about with their outward expression of contentment and total willingness to serve.

It did not look natural somehow, and on looking back I have finally figured out what was missing with those women and girls. Not one of them exhibited any outward sign of a personality.

Anything of a personal nature was always guarded. In any such expression, they seemed to require the approval of a man of their congregation if one was present, and one or more men seemed always to be with them – we never saw a female alone. On those rare occasions when it was possible to talk briefly with one of them, before they would talk to any of us, even to say "hello" in answer to our "hello," they would have to look for approval toward one or the other of their church men.

Church masters more like.

If it was an occasion that normally would allow for laughter, it was always cut short. If by chance all the men were responding favorably to whatever the amusement was, the women and girls would then seem to embrace the frivolity. But this was usually cut short, as there always seemed to be something that suddenly needed to be picked up, moved around, straightened up, hung up – or perhaps there were just flies that needed to be shooed away. These people stayed busy; it was almost as if they were racing against the clock, or waiting for something they expected to happen.

Of course, we did not know it then, but we were witnessing the so-called first boot drop, and these people knew we did not know what was going on. They were waiting for the next boot to fall, and they would not have to wait long. By the end of August of that year, 1942, all the ticky-tacky houses were built, about fifty, all it seemed on land owned by Denny Mitchell. The houses surrounded a rather ostentatious tabernacle church, completely finished inside and out and with no expense spared, as country churches go.

It was truly the grandest we had ever seen. The houses, some with picket fences and painted in church colors – purple and white – were quite the sight. When all that was done, more of these people came, at least a hundred and fifty, moving in. The initial group, who had done all the work, were suddenly up and gone. We never knew where, and at first we hardly knew they had left.

Slowly we would come to know.

As hard as it had been to approach the recently departed, these new arrivals were as different from them as night to day. They seemed to wallow in friendliness, and I had not seen so much handshaking going on since old Willard Memfrees ran for Sheriff of Dunklin County.

One might say they were friendly to a fault, but not without a purpose. They came to the Bootheel of Southeast Missouri with a mission, and within a month, they had that mission up and running. It was executed so smoothly that I do not think any of us locals were aware of what was really going on. These new religious arrivals virtually bowled us over from the moment they settled into our community.

They began to move into those ticky-tacky houses that we supposed the first bunch had built for them.

It was not much more than a month from the time they arrived in our community that they were the community. We thought, well how do you like that?

At least they had money and in many ways, they became the movers and shakers. They were the hub of our society, and everything seemed to hum around this church body and Mr. Denny Mitchell.

Eventually we could see the plot begin to thicken. They had certainly brought with them a new idea of advocating a most radical change in the direction our little cross-roads was heading – which admittedly was nowhere – and what took place next took us all by storm. They set their church members up on that quota arrangement I mentioned before – the one for bringing in newcomers and getting their fancy robes. They expressed an urgent need to add to the flock again, as if running against the clock. And that's just what they were doing, because for their elaborate scheme to work, they had meet their deadline. They needed to add at least fifty-one percent of the people in Southeast Missouri to their congregation by election time two years hence.

They pulled out all the stops, gave to their church

members the authority to speak for the church in offering those selected for membership in this beautiful tabernacle, twenty-five acres of good farm land, complete with a new ticky-tacky house and furniture. They even included a team of mules with a harness, a cultivator, harrow, disc and seed planter that could be easily converted from cotton to corn.

They also arranged for the mail to be delivered three times a week, rather than only once – if we were lucky. All of that was promised, with the church holding power of attorney for all such selected members, using that as the power of a voting bloc – legal and binding, mind you. We would be joining the church, supported and sponsored by it. They would begin advocating in every way for changes for the good of all people.

With the power of this new voting bloc, the church could request electricity to be brought to our community, as well as the telephone. To us it seemed too good to be true – and it was, but at the time, who knew. None of us for an instant had ever owned a piece of land, let alone a house, and now this miracle was happening right before our eyes.

Naturally, everyone was converting, to get in on a good thing while it lasted, not being bothered by the small print on those power of attorney documents. We did not know anything about legal contracts and such. We all reassured ourselves that since Mr. Denny seemed to know what was going on, surely he would tell us if everything was not on the up and up. Oh, we would learn better.

Ch. 9: Tenant Farmers Get To Own Land

Right at that time, this religious order began to do what we called a land office business. I am quite sure they thought about everything they might run into. I imagine they had planned each eventuality, what they might encounter by way of resistance and how to deal with it.

I think the one thing they never fully anticipated was the overwhelmingly favorable response everyone gave to what this church and its officials were espousing.

This would all very shortly become unacceptable to the Great General American Land Company, which owned thousands and thousands of acres in Dunklin County, which was just across the road from Pemberscott County, where all of this activity was taking place. It was the sharecroppers in Dunklin County – which many of us were – that the church had targeted for conversion.

This move, coming on the heels of a major desertion of the company store by the tenant farmers who took their trade to Gobler instead – well, this marked Mr. Denny for special attention from no less than the Ku Klux Klan. The church's offer of land that we would own, however, was having an effect on these hard working people. They were dizzy with the wonder of it all, but there was some bad trouble brewing in Paradise.

It did not take long for the dreaded Klan to come onto the scene. They started their campaign of harassment and threats against us poor sharecroppers who were leaving the land owned by the great General American Land Company, for most of us were nothing more than indentured laborers.

The company had grown rich from our labor over the years and arrogant towards us. The company kept us under their control, in part through our debt to the company store. We could never seem to pay it off because we were never allowed to keep our own books. Some of us did open those books, but in secret, and those who did knew that the company's figures and ours never matched. They were robbing us blind. They slid the scales in the field to get more from us and took more by overcharging in the company store.

They saw that they could do it, and we could not do a thing about it – so they thought. If we wanted to continue living on their land, we had to accept it. If we did not like how things were, or if they did not like how we were doing things, hundreds of people out of work or a place to live were waiting to replace us.

They spread this lie, thinking we did not know our value to them. They believed they had us conditioned to accept things as they were, thus assuring they could continue to get away with this perpetual theft. However, everyone involved in sharing these ill-gotten gains had become dependent on their scheme. When so many of us began to respond to the offer of land from this new church, given an offer we could not refuse, few did refuse.

It put everything in a new light and exposed the lie that we could be quickly replaced, that no one would miss us. Their fear of us leaving in mass was plain to see by the actions of the Klan, for shortly after this began, mystery followed mystery. The new prefabricated houses that were built so quickly began mysteriously to burn as well.

Ch. 10: The Klan Makes Itself Known

When the Klan first came calling, we all remembered that the Company said this might happen if we went through with moving out.

They did not say how they knew, just that it might. The thing that had the most chilling effect on us was the way in which their spokesman hurled that torch down at our feet as they were leaving. We knew who he was under that sheet, the foreman and land overseer that we had had to deal with on a less-than-friendly basis at least one day a month, year after year. Before, he had control and was sure of himself. Now, he was hiding under a sheet, standing there backed up by at least fifty or more fellow Klan members.

They looked unreal – almost stupid, strange as that sounds. We could tell he was frustrated, thrown off his game. I am sure it was the first time in his miserable life that his employers had told him to get some of his Brotherhood together, ride out to the county line and put a stop to us jumping ship.

At the same time, the Company had to make it all look trivial, so as not to overly alarm their foreman. Therefore, they treated the whole thing as an off-hand matter, of little or no consequence. Only, it was big, very big. No amount of assurance to the contrary would change the fact that a new player had come into the game, with his own cards and own rules to play by.

For whatever reason, it seemed all this fuss, one way or the other, was about us. We were about to go from being unimportant to being something to die for.

The big old land company was king, but this religious body was far bigger. In fact, to fight their way to prominence they now enjoyed on the world stage, they were suspected of resorting to killing certain opposition in their early days. This was not an isolated occurrence. They employed many questionable tactics to get their way and to dominate every facet of life. They had started when this was not yet a state, took over and carved out what would become a state. They elected judges, mayors and governors with their religious and political influence.

But the Great General American Land Company was out of their league in this contest.

All of these initial local skirmishes between the church and these land barons were pretty well kept out of the public's eye.

We did not have roving reporters in them days, so this policy of one bad turn deserves another went on until something terrible happened. Of course, I guess that would really depend on whom you asked.

Finally, a Klansman, our overseer's brother, himself as well as his wife and another person one could identify, were burned beyond recognition. They were the victims of a bad car wreck, slamming into a bridge coming out of Kennett. Seemed the damn thing exploded on contact and burned everybody up.

It all looked very suspicious, and so quiet – naturally the fingers pointing and whispering about it to one another almost became a pastime. Since that accident took place, there was now genuine fear that we were somehow mixed up in something dangerous. To us it all seemed to stem from these new seekers of Zion and our involvement with them, for our own good, of course. We certainly were not comfortable worshiping inside that ostentatious purple and white mausoleum, the Tabernacle of the Saints of the New Zion Church. We felt out of place and thought it was rather grand – that is to say, rather gaudy. We had never seen the likes of it.

Anyway, all this happened, and then some other things took place that had some unsettling overtones. So the great opportunity that so many had excitedly taken advantage of slowly began to lose its luster. We wondered what we had gotten ourselves into; finally, we admitted to each other that we felt openly uneasy. This was a new fear for us, and we sought comfort in one another by making flippant remarks about our fears. Our fears, however, were well founded. In addition to the overseer's brother, we had three houses and a cotton wagon, tarp and all, that mysteriously burned to the ground. No one was in the houses, but they had already been assigned to new converts.

The cotton wagon had been a different matter. An itinerant man by the name of Barlow Skinner was asleep in the cotton wagon. He escaped with his life, but breathed so much smoke that he will never be good for any kind of work. His hair had caught fire and the folks who tried to help him had trouble catching him. It was especially bad because he had been lying there naked, just covered with the cotton and that tarp. Seemed he had taken off his overalls and washed them in the water trough to clean them as best he could.

He washed his overalls every two weeks, he said, whether they needed it or not. He was quick to point out that he used no soap, so that no harm would come to the mules who would need to drink the water. We all knew that more than likely he just did not own a bar of soap. As a matter of fact, the only thing he owned was his trusty Ronson lighter. It seemed to fascinate him, even though he had long since worn out the flint. He treasured it nonetheless.

Now this poor fellow was seriously hurt. He was addled of mind, badly burned, with scars on his head, face and upper body. Almost as hurtful to Skinner was that now his cigarette lighter was missing. But he had survived and could still get around surprisingly well. He would ask almost everyone he saw, "Did you see who done it?" When we said we had not, he would say in an understanding tone, "I know."

It did not matter who was talking with whom or where he would happen to be. He would jump in with his question, and we would answer. It was sad to behold, but that was not to be the end of it. It was just the opening salvo, for there were so many different undercurrents of passion both religious and political. All these different, dearly held beliefs were backed by some very heavy breathers, who had to win at all costs. And there we were caught in the middle, we flat landers, not knowing who were the bad guys. At that point, we could not even answer Barlow Skinner's question.

Ch. 11: Mr. Denny Plans A Fair

For the next few days, everything seemed to be cooling off some; we heard of no more mischief. Things were quiet for the better part of two weeks and then the people on County Line Road received some news that would serve to push everything else to the back burner. Mr. Denny received a reply to his request from the County Fair Committee to hold the fair there at Gobler. He had said he had everything in the way of facilities, and if by some chance he needed something more, by damn he would get it. After all, that was what he was known for.

Well, the answer from this committee, four in all, three women and one man, was that they would come and look the place over. In the next few weeks, they would come and visit Gobler. So he hired a few of us locals to set to work on that road, getting all the remaining trees, stumps and brush pulled up and blasted out.

We pushed them together, burned them and hauled them off. When the trucks of dirt came in, we leveled that area off and graveled over the packed-down earth. We also dug a good-sized ditch on each side. It was a nice improvement. Then the prison trucks, with the guard and convicts, showed up with two more loads of convicts to work on the racetrack. The convicts would work on one section, while the rest of us would work on another. We whipped it into shape.

We left part of it as a mud track and hard packed the

rest. On part of the track we laid large logs across, about every fifty feet or so. The horses would have to jump these, and we all agreed that the layout offered a challenge to horse and rider. It also had a street that had to be negotiated with a steep bank on the far side.

Last but not least was the slough itself, what most called a swamp. We cleared out most of the obvious problems. The water was not deep when you entered. About halfway in it, the water would come up to the knee of a full-grown horse. There may have been snakes, but we could not say for sure. We doubted it, but common sense dictated that they probably were there.

Crawdads built their castles here. We tried to tear them down, but they would build them up overnight, so we left them alone.

When it was finally time to walk that layout, we nailed large signs to trees along the track so riders could see how far they had gone. Mr. Denny paid three men out of Deering to survey the track, and they figured it for just over three miles, about thirty feet wide in most parts. We all thought Mr. Denny Mitchell had it about right.

There were also games to establish and lay out. We would have the slick tree climb, foot racing, the axe throw, the pole toss, a shooting challenge for marksmen only, and other games as well. Then of course there would be the judging of everything from jellies and jams to cakes, cookies and pretzels.

There would be every kind of sausage known to man as

well as blood pudding, hogs-head cheese, and a real southern dish called tripe.

I do believe there must have been at least fifty different recipes of that alone that were entered for judging. I pitied the poor judges in that category, not to mention in the blood pudding and the hogs-head cheese judging.

As far as why there were so many entries for things like blood pudding, hogs-head cheese, and the like, why, it was just that back then nothin', and I mean *nothin'* went to waste if we could help it. That was a thrifty trait come over from Europe and the British Isles from our ancestors, many of whom were some of those pleasant peasants we speak of on other pages of this book, and who needed to save every last morsel of anything that could nourish the human body.

So blood, for instance, something people with more wherewithal might have just thrown away - I mean, *blood*, for goodness sake, became the main ingredient for a savory dish, blood pudding. A lot of times it had bread crumbs or oatmeal in it to hold it together, and often it had its own casing of intestine, because in truth it was a kind of sausage.

Now the hogs-head cheese, or just head cheese as some called it, was more of a terrine, if you want to get fancy-dancy Frenchy about it, made out of spices, chopped vegetables, pigs' feet and the broth from them (for the gel that kept the whole thing together as it cooled), and a whole lot of spices. Of course, there wasn't one bit of real cheese in there, and to be sure, I don't know why it was ever called cheese, maybe because it was eaten when there wasn't any real cheese to be found.

Another reason for all these sausage-type dishes was that if you put enough vinegar, spices, sugar or salt, etc., into them, they lasted a good bit of time without refrigeration – or maybe all those things just covered up the fetid taste and smell when they were startin' to turn!

But at this fair, tripe was King. I've heard it called "edible offal" because of being made from the first three chambers of the cow's (or sheep's or goat's) stomach, but having tasted it, I've often wondered if someone didn't mean "edible awful"!

I've heard it said tripe is eaten in some form all over the world and all I have to say is, if that's true, there must be some hungry people out there.

Well it was just like the man said – if he did not have what was needed, he would build it, buy it or do whatever it took to get it. With that kind of support for their fair, the august body of citizens making up the committee was only too glad, or should I say honored, to award the location of the fair for the year of nineteen hundred and forty two to Mr. Denny Mitchell and his new township of Gobler, Missouri.

Ch. 12: There's Gamblin' At The Fair!

This news was almost the equivalent of announcing to us that the war was over. Well, maybe not really, but this was something for us. We needed this diversion; we felt that this more than anything else put us on the map and made us feel special. This is just my way of saying that this was earth-shaking news to us. We could not imagine that our own little neck of the woods would hold the fair this year, or any other year as for that matter.

Our very own County Fair!

We owed it all to Mr. Denny Mitchell.

Now the fair was set to open the first week in October of that year. Fliers went out all over the place announcing that our fair would welcome everyone from far and near. This alone was different as in the past our County Fairs catered mostly to the folks of our county. Mr. Denny had it announced on several well-known radio stations, including the money prizes to be given to the winners of the different events. He talked about arm wrestling, broad jumps, the fifty-yard dash, greased pig wrestling, horseshoe tossing, etc.

Of course, he mentioned the horse races. There was only a small fee to enter any of these contests. There was weight guessing, age guessing and married or single. Mr. Denny had set this all up to make money. Every game there would be self-supporting, and everyone who was put in charge of all these different events volunteered. Since it was for the community, inspired and sponsored by a man well known to us all, Mr. Denny Mitchell, every one complied. A community spirit overtook everyone such that within two days of the fair actually opening, our old County Line Road was throwing up a continuous rooster tail of yellow dust caused by cars and trucks of every make and model, with many pulling some fancy horse trailers. They were making their way on down to Gobler, wanting to be first to arrive to get the best parking.

Now it seemed to us country folk to be a continuous upwelling of dust. I do believe there were people coming down our road from several states around.

Such crowds were turning out as were rarely seen at a County Fair. I think we even had people from the State Fair committees, maybe even for World's Fairs and such.

Well, it could have been.

There was going to be some major horseracing and wagering going on too. Mr. Denny was going to make sure that while there might never be a second fair at his place, he at least was going to give the people one they would never forget. And that he did. What we did not know was that he was transforming this not so idyllic Eden into what was fast turning out to be, though still thinly disguised as a County Fair, a very professionally run gambling operation.

We were victims of having been misguided. Now whether through a deliberate intent or it just turned out that way, it did not really make any difference. Many big bets were going to be placed, and Mr. Denny was going to cover them all.

Now can you imagine the good Christian men and women who volunteered to work those different booths for Mr. Denny? They did not seem to make the connection that they were acting as the fronts for something illegal.

We were all so taken with Mr. Denny. How he operated everything that he was connected with seemed new and exciting to us. We were almost too willing to get involved in anything that he seemed to indicate was a good thing. Now it should be said on his behalf, none of us could actually say that he told us to do anything, neither one way or the other; but he seemed to be rich and what's more, he seemed to be getting richer. Lord knows we were taken in by this; we forgot that appearances can be misleading.

Add to this the fact that he was a complete paradox. We would later learn of the terrible pressure he was under. The kind of pressure that would already have broken the average person, and adding to that, he was now having a complete change of heart about, and regret for what was now becoming an impossible position to maintain or justify. Through the genuine love we had shown to Mr. Denny and his family, he began to have honest-to-goodness misgivings about the decisions he had made out of the belief that there was no other way. He had believed he was acting out of necessity, but whatever the real reason he had changed his mind, he realized he had made a terrible decision and his heart was no longer in it. He had begun to think of us as his friends, and now knew that he could no longer keep up this charade. He wanted so much to come clean, to get it off his chest and be the man that we all believed he was.

But how to do this, that was the rub. He had no one he could turn to; his loving wife was not aware of the terrible alliance he had with these builders of their New Zion, or how they were in reality politically allied with the Nazis. All the while these Zionists were vying for world power through religious rule that they believed would be bestowed on them if Hitler was victorious with his new World Order.

It was a real mess and very dangerous both for his wife and son, as well as for him. Not to mention his brother and several uncles and aunts in Ireland that he believed were being held hostage by the Nazis to assure he would follow their orders.

He thought back to when and how he had been pulled into this. It was only two years ago, and was it really because of those reasons? Was it fear for the safety of his relatives? Was it fear of what might happen to his own family?

Fear of this, fear of that, fear of the unknown. Fear makes a man do many things.

Though I think, it was really nothing less than the

blackmail. At first, there had been something in it for him, like that key connection he had been put in touch with in Chicago.

Man had called himself Metzger, and it was through Metzger that he placed all his orders for merchandise and never asked questions about how Metzger was able to deliver anything and everything he ordered. That Metzger was the assistant manager of the Chicago Trade Mall probably had something to do with it. Secretly, Mr. Denny enjoyed his new elevated status, solely because of being able to deliver.

He had also become accustomed to playing the role of hero to these poor farmers. He knew they were good, hardworking people who trusted him, looked up to him, and needed him. More the truth, he probably needed them even more than they needed him. Without him realizing it, the truth surfaced. They were now his people, and this was his home. While at first he had simply followed what seemed the path of least resistance, all that was light years behind him now.

Now he had to admit to himself the real reason that he had gotten involved with those godless Nazi creatures. It was just plain greed and vanity, and now that he finally admitted it to himself, he was already beginning to feel better. With that realization, he began to arm himself with a new determination to get right with himself, God and his fellow man.

No more lies to himself about the path of least resistance. As for the threat they placed on his head to keep him in line, well, that he would challenge. What did those swine think they were going to pull off? He must have been crazy to allow them to think that a sorry bunch of Nazis could push around Denny Mitchell. Here in this country?

No, in his country. Mr. Denny was surprised at the good feeling he had when he realized this was his country too.

Denny Mitchell said, "I must have been crazy, but I ain't no more! Let them take their so-called instructions and shove 'em in their ear."

Well, maybe he did not say it quite like that, but you get my meaning.

They had told him that as long as he followed instructions and did just what he was told, that no harm would come to him or his family. Up until now, he had done just that. Now he was fighting mad. He had finally come to his senses and would no longer be overcome with a dread foreboding.

He had thrown himself into the work of setting up Gobler, poor choice of words perhaps, of making it ready for the County Fair. As he set about this work, a plan of sorts began to materialize for him. The more he thought about it, the more he came to believe that it might just work.

He had used several thousand dollars – twenty-plus, at least – to build this place. He never allowed himself to reflect on the sordid truth that this money was a part of the millions upon millions that the Nazis had stolen from the Jews they had murdered – yes, he heard those stories too. It was this twenty thousand-plus dollars that they had furnished him to buy the land and build up Gobler. He knew he was really building it for them, but of course he had not allowed himself to dwell on that either.

He had also used several thousand more, about two to be exact, to bribe the warden in charge of the Missouri State Penitentiary, so that he could use convict labor. Supposedly said labor was free, but of course, it cost him the two thousand dollars to arrange, albeit through the money that the Nazis had sent him. It was also not free to those men who had been killed.

Now he was going to use still more of it to pay the Warden once again. He needed additional use of the prisoners to complete his plan. He felt that he had to do this one more time, and thinking about it again tended to make him feel sick. He knew the deaths were unnecessary.

How could those unfortunate prisoners on thick chains have been a threat to the guards? If he could put this plan of his in place, while he could never bring back those two lost prisoners, it was possible that he could raise the money needed to pay back his brother in Ireland.

He was not sure, of course, if he could get that Nazi bunch there to accept the money back and let him off the hook. His hopes might not have been realistic, but he wanted to appeal to their good graces to let his family there return it. I am not sure what he expected to happen. Perhaps out of the goodness of their hearts they would see what he had done and let his people go.

In his heart he knew they would not, but he was desperate. He knew he had to try.

Ch. 13: The Klan/Irish Plot Thickens

Denny's brother was named Timothy O'Mitcheler, and he was the go-between for the Nazis. According to him, his family were being held captive for this very purpose, to handle transactions between them in Ireland and Mr. Denny Mitchell or anyone else here in the United States. It was a near-perfect plan, designed for secrecy and efficiency.

Oh, how sweet that must have been for them, to control one or two families in Ireland with relatives in the United States. Kidnap them, threaten them with bodily harm if their demands were not met.

After that, it was just a matter of bringing the person into the camp, instructing him and sending him the money to do his work. Use contacts here to observe him and make reports back on what he was doing. Make sure that he was doing everything he was instructed to do.

They checked other things as well, like his attitude, his loyalty and his determination. Oh, Denny Mitchell knew they were watching him. He just did not know who was watching. So far the most important instructions he had received was to purchase enough land to be seen as a man of means. He had to give the appearance of being successful, so he set himself up in business to become a leader of the community. They even told him where they wanted him to buy the land and from whom.

Yes, he knew without a doubt that he was under

scrutiny. To tell the truth, he just could not understand how these Nazis knew about those old eccentric hermits. He did wonder what their part amounted to in this subversion.

Then he remembered what it was that had bothered him the most about that old lean-to, what had seemed out of place when he had first seen it. There was a rather high antenna coming out of the back of that thing that, on thinking about it, had no logical reason for being there.

Unless…

Mr. Denny had pushed that thought aside. *Lord, I've begun to suspect everyone.* Then the thought popped into his head, what if they were part of it all? Because he did not know for sure, he thought it best to err on the side of caution. If they were in on it, those old boys were probably in regular contact with that submarine, the one that locals had seen at the mouth of the Mississippi River. That realization floored him, for that would mean that informants and agents literally surrounded him.

There would be no better place to set up a short-wave transmitter than among a bunch of flatland dirt farmers, as we were. Put it down deep in some god-awful swamp, such as where those two old hermits were. How much better it was for them to keep an eye on the progress of their own agent, Mr. Denny Mitchell himself. Buy the land from the two as he had done, start the project involving all of them. Put everything into motion so that it would appear everything was on track or even ahead of schedule. Mr. Denny felt that any reports sent so far would say so, and he was right. Reports had been sent, and special instructions had come back.

Mr. Denny was to expect a special package that would be sent general delivery to the post office in Kennett, addressed to him. He was to follow the instructions just as they were in the package.

The package arrived. He picked it up and found the first installment of money, all very illicit-like, almost enough to arouse suspicion, with a letter telling him of the sender's desire to come to America. After the war, he wanted Mr. Denny to invest this money in some land for him, and there would follow additional funds later for this purpose. In a postscript, added to look like an afterthought, the letter instructed him to get in touch with one Bishop Monsignor O'Malley, who was in charge of the religious body that would be moving into Southeast Missouri in the very near future.

That is the story of how he came to be involved in this sorry mess. Now Mr. Denny was beginning to see a way to extricate himself from that bunch of vipers, straighten out his life and regain some self-respect.

What of this plan, then?

It was all right there under his nose. Mr. Denny Mitchell would cultivate the animosity between the Great General American Land Company and the movers and shakers holding themselves forth as a devout religious order. Oh, he knew the Company was nothing more than tyrants toward us tenant farmers for all those years, so a large part of this fight he was going to bring to the Company would be striking a blow on our behalf, as it were. He knew the so-called religious order was even stonier than those land barons, and though he himself was not clean, he was going to get clean. If possible, he was going to bring down both Goliaths of greed and corruption at the same time, though he realized this was going to be one hell of a disruption of the status quo.

He also knew he would never have a better opportunity than the recognition of just how deeply this one bunch resented the other. They opted to help things along towards what he felt was an inevitable outcome. Alone, he would fan the flames of animosity between the two. He had no way at the time of knowing that he was going to have much help to that end. To wit, the acts of arson and threats that had already started, that Mr. Denny had nothing to do with. He may not have started it, but he did mean to see it finished.

For now, there was much to do. This fair was but another piece of his plan, and the time was at hand for him to capitalize on his knowledge of human nature. He knew that man had a tendency to want to gamble. Though he knew it was illegal, the fair was only for a week and he was counting on everyone thinking the authorities had approved it all. Some of them had even entered the horse races, especially the big one set for Saturday for the quarter horses.

Mr. Denny knew that the quarter horses could reach their top speed in the first thirty feet off the start line and that sometimes this speed exceeded thirty miles an hour.

Now this was another event where a huge attendance was expected. Because it was a race where everyone could see the entire event and because the race was only a quarter mile, with the horses running top speed in the first thirty feet, it was quite the sight to see. So quick off the line were some of these quarter horses that many inexperienced riders were thrown off. In some cases, even experienced riders were unceremoniously dumped off backwards. Many lost their hats and their composure at the same time.

You see, on takeoff you have to lean forward as far as you can. Woe unto the uninitiated who does not heed the advice to grab hold of the reins firmly and saddle horn tightly. You do your best to hold onto your seat, your head and, if possible, your hat. If you have to lose something, though, it is probably best you lose the hat.

I think we can all agree on that. These horses were bred for working cattle, so they were fast from the get-go in order to cut in and out of cattle and get the cowboy where he needed to be at a moment's notice.

The races were short, fast and over quickly, making it possible for several to run in one afternoon. You knew quickly if your horse won or lost, and if you won money or not.

It was a fun sport for the spectators and riders. We believed the horses rather enjoyed it too.

Ch. 14: Let The Bells Ring!

Our fair was underway with a great send-off. From the opening bell, everything about the fair was in harmony. Mr. Denny had arranged to signal the start of this momentous event by the ringing of many bells of different shapes and sizes. All of the cotton farmers had a bell of some kind, and that is what they supplied. Individuals who operated different concessions had cow bells, dinner bells and brass and iron bells. Others had copper bells. Some were tiny, and a few were very large.

Let there be no doubt about it, this was a very happy time for all of us. We did not dare believe that this would ever actually happen, but here were the County Fair and the bells.

Each concessionaire kept the bell at the post, and we all heard them ringing joyously off and on throughout the days of our fair, whenever the Spirit moved them.

That set the tone for the good times. Everybody seemed to love ringing those bells, if just for the sheer exuberance of doing so. I recommend trying it sometime. If you do not have a bell, grab a drum and flail away on it. You will feel that same joy everyone felt at the fair.

Now there was not the first security guard or any other lawman, except of course for our local Sheriff. He was only there for show. The Great General American Land Company, which owned him, told him to make a few PR appearances. They knew we all suspected him of being a member of the Klan, and with the election coming might help him garner some votes.

Other lawmen may have been there as well, I do not know.

I do know that we had never in our lives seen so many people, and they did not look poor like us.

Well, some might have, but mostly they acted different, looked different and talked different. They were, as I said, different.

They came there from all over and for sure quite a few of those men smelled as if they had just left a barbershop. I must tell you that some of those women dressed, well, almost funny. They dressed different, to say the least. I finally got up the nerve to ask a man about what one woman was wearing. I believe he had said, "Oh, she's gotta habit." I swear to me it sounded like he said, "Oh, she's gotta have it."

Ch. 15: Miss Sonja Henie Arrives

It was the funny way they talked. I stood there watching people stroll by when this very nice looking young woman walked up to me and asked where she might find the "necessaries." I scratched my head and tried to act intelligent as I studied on what she said. I noticed she was dressed in a like manner as the other woman I had inquired about.

It dawned on me that she had a habit herself – or she's gotta have it. Since I did not know what kind of habit she had, I did not know what she had to have.

I did, however, believe that it all had something to do with those funny looking britches they were all wearing. I did not know what the necessaries were that she was looking for. I asked her what it was she had to have, and how bad she had to have it. We did not have any of necessaries, or whatever she called them, that I knew of.

I was just trying to sound sympathetic and to draw out the conversation with her because she sure was pretty.

She hit me with the padded piece of leather she had been slapping her leg with and went off looking for someone to report me to. Those people were just plumb strange. I chalked it up to them having money. I did get a laugh later when she met up with another like-minded woman. They both looked at me, turned in a huff, and walked on down the trail. I suppose they were looking for whatever it was that women dressed like that had to have. All they were going to find in the direction they headed, however, were the rest stations Mr. Denny had set up.

He had put them up all over the place. Mr. Denny called them rest stations. Others called them toilets or vestibules, which was close enough.

We local boys liked to call them crappers, which tended to get the meaning across. That woman's request did not fall within the parameters of my understanding. One thing I knew for sure was that she definitely was not going to find any – what did she call them, necessaries – down there.

I did not understand why she had gotten so mad in the first place, just because I did not know the answer to her question about finding her necessaries. No one ever told me about them, so how was I supposed to know. She certainly did not have to hit me. It hurt like the blue blazes, but she was pretty and she smelled pretty too. My uncle told me later that most women who have money have perfume and that was probably what she had. At the time, I thought that if the perfume was what made her so mad, then I would prefer to be around girls who wore sachets any time.

Of course, I was only ten, and some said I acted young for my age. I did not know anything at all about girls and women, or anything like that.

From this experience, coupled with the little exposure I had to the women of this new Church, I concluded easily that women who dressed funny as these women attending our fair did were showing a sure sign of having to have something. They had to have it, and they could only find it at a place called "the necessaries."

Oh, I am sure that where she was from, that was just the way one asked about it. Here in Southeast Missouri, we had never heard of such things. I had to laugh at myself again. My cheek was swollen up, but boy, she sure was pretty.

I thought to myself that if she came back my way and I could smell that perfume again, well, I would not mind letting her take another swipe at me.

It did not happen just like that, but she did show up again. This time there was a man with her. They stood around acting natural and stopped down past me a ways. He came back alone and asked me, "Boy, what did you say to my wife a little earlier?"

I said to him, somewhat scared now, "Sir, I do not know."

He told me not to be afraid, that I could tell him. He did appear sincere. He told me that his wife had said something he could not make sense of. He motioned her to come back and told me to just tell them both what I said and why. So I did, going back to the point where I had asked the one gentleman about the clothes another lady was wearing. She was dressed in the same manner as his wife. They looked funny – to me, they looked strange at least.

Before I had finished, they were both laughing. He put his arm around me like a pal, one might say, and asked me my name. I told him Bobby Snow Wiltshire.

He repeated my name and introduced his wife, Mrs. Sonja Henie. I offered my hand to her, but instead she hugged me and kissed my swollen cheek, saying repeatedly how sorry she was that she had been angry with me.

The smell of her hair and the wonder of her were almost more than my little brain could compute. For sure, the circuits were all overloaded.

Remember, I was only ten.

I know they were both amused by how backward I was, at least I thought so. They told me they were driving back to a place called Hollywood, where Mrs. Henie was a movie star, and asked me if I knew what that was.

Thank God, I knew that, or else they would have known how ignorant we country folk were.

I remember feeling like I saved the day for us by knowing what a movie star was. What I did not know was that a movie star could be either a man, a woman, or even a dog. I do not think they knew I did not know that.

As I am sure you know, Mrs. Sonja Henie made it back to Hollywood, where she made it big time in the movies. She had been discovered when she won a gold medal in the Olympics for figure skating, representing her home country of Sweden. She then went on to win the hearts of people all over the world.

That day, she made another conquest – me. She had the heart of a small country boy who had slipped off from the cotton patch where he was supposed to be pulling bolls.

I've been wondering ever since then just what it was about Mrs. Henie that made me a 10-year-old gibbering idiot in her presence – why, I guess it's just that she was the most beautiful thing I had ever seen, and not only that. Coupled with that beauty (now picture this – hair the color of the palest taffy and all done up in what they called Marcelled style, with the waves kinda crimped in to call attention to the face, why it was kinda old-fashioned, but on her it also managed to be the highest kind of nowadays beauty, now what that hair really did was call attention to her face, with its lightly applied makeup and eye ornamentation for brows and eyelashes just enough to make them stand out, and then to bring into the limelight – 'cause she was an actress, a performer after all – those lips: the cherry on the most sublime sundae ever concocted by God and man. Those were what we called Cupie-doll lips, after that little doll, who, after all, actually looked like Mrs. Henie, not the other way around) and a tendency to be pretty nice and pleasant even after she thought I had slandered her in some way – why I was bumfuzzled by the very thought of her, let alone her actual presence standing there before me in little God-forsaken Gobler in Southeast Missouri.

But to get back to earlier in that day, I had shucked that cotton sack, got the strap from around my shoulder, and left the whole thing laying right there in the cotton row. I had run like a rabbit all the way to the fair, about three miles. The rest of the short time that they spent with me that wonderful day became a blur in my memory.

I soon realized I had to get back and get to work hauling bolls, or I would have to face my Dad. They put me into the most beautiful automobile in the world and rushed me back. I got out on the road, waved goodbye, and turned and ran lickety-split over to where I had left my cotton sack. I found it and quickly got back in the harness, so to speak, proceeding to fill up my sack by stripping stalks from the bottom up.

The cotton had already been picked, and what was left was just dried up cotton balls. Since they still had some cotton left, not much to be sure, we could gather it up or it would be plowed under. The whole time I did some rethinking about that perfume versus sachet business. As I was lugging my full sack of bolls to the wagon, it hit me that my mother, grandmother, sister and aunts all wore sachet. My uncle confirmed later that women with money wore perfume while those without, our women folk, wore sachet.

I thought if ours were women, what did that make Mrs. Sonja Henie? She was certainly a woman too, but suddenly I was finding it very difficult to follow such logic. She sure did not look or talk like Mother or Grandmother. For that matter, she did not talk like my aunts. She gave me a weird feeling that was all too new to me, and last but not least, she did not smell like Mother, Grandmother or any other person of the feminine persuasion that I had ever known. Please do remember I was only ten, and do not judge me too harshly.

My uncle was the only person I ever told of my exciting experience. It turned out he thought I was lying, so he never bothered to speak of it to my dad or mother.

There was, though, that bit of lipstick on my face and the bruise under my eye, which did not hardly hurt by the time I was home. There was also that lingering aroma of what we connoisseurs – that is, men of the world – would know to be very expensive perfume, the kind only the Sonja Henies of the world, or women with money, would ever be able to wear.

Later we heard rumors, well all the radio shows were talking about it, that our Miss Sonja was gaga over that showman of all showmen, Liberace. Stop, you say – that doesn't seem quite right. Oh they were both pretty enough – in fact, he was almost prettier than she was, with more makeup, a bigger and more flamboyant hairstyle, elevator shoes (okay, I don't really know about that, didn't see 'em myself or to tell the truth even hear of them from the radio rumormongers, but it would fit the picture wouldn't it?), those clothes he wore, mostly for his later Las Vegas shows, all after the time of good ol' Gobler and its fair. But you know, those radio announcers, I think they made up a good lot of that stuff just to keep us folks in the boonies talking about their show and what we heard on it! As for our Miss

Sonja and Mr. Liberace, well, it could have been true, couldn't it.

But once again to get back to what was going on in the world at that time, I am sure that I was missing something else in all of it. I thought at the time that life was wonderful. There was also at that time another tug of war raging, and this one would shortly break out into full-blown disaster. I will tell you about it, but I think that first I should mention about the stranger.

Ch. 16: A Stranger Comes To The Fair

The stranger showed up looking rather disheveled and unkempt, with a stooped bearing and an odd-looking pair of glasses, with wire rims. He needed a shave and looked kind of dirty, wearing an old soiled, long-sleeved shirt, rolled up sleeves, green in color with lighter green pants and red suspenders so dirty they were almost black. This was topped off with a black soiled-looking toboggan pulled down over dark red shaggy hair much in need of a trimming. He spoke with a brogue that we would later come to learn was Irish-English.

He started making inquiries of a most peculiar nature. From time to time, he would ask where he might find "Laddie Boy." He insisted that we should know the Lad he was looking for. He was supposed to be known around here, that we might know him as Denehaee O'Mitchelers.

After a while some of us picked up on this and asked "Do you mean Mr. Denny Mitchell?"
"So that's what you call him," the stranger said. "So then where can I find this, what do you call him, Denny Mitchell is it?"

Well, we told him to just go out to County Line Road and follow the traffic east. It would lead right into Gobler, and he could join in the fair and would find Mr. Denny. So the fellow said, "Top o'th'mornin' to ya!" and set off, as he said, to find his brother.

With the coming of this rather brash, uncouth-appearing stranger, Mr. Denny's brother no less, Mr. Denny would learn some devastating news. At the same time, it was news that would free him from the clutches of the Nazis: his relatives in Ireland were dead.

This man looked older than he actually was. In all truth, Mr. Denny did not recognize him at first. But he was in fact his brother, only three years older than Mr. Denny. He managed to escape his captors and survive, making his way to the safety of this country and to his brother's protection.

Alas, there was danger a-plenty here too, even in a place where it was not expected. You cannot imagine how this man's coming would affect us all that fall.

It is also for certain that this man, brother or no, had brought his own trouble with him. It would not take long before that trouble would show itself.

Now America had been attacked one year earlier, December 7, 1941, to be exact. Our naval base at Pearl Harbor had sustained a devastating blow as the result of a cowardly sneak attack by the military might of the Japanese Imperial Navy and Air Force. Though we did not yet know it, Hitler was about to join with Japan and declare war on us as well. Things were heating up all over the place.

Our big sprawling County Fair with all its many diversions would be the last hurrah for us until this terrible war was won. Even though we were told many times in so many ways by our War Correspondents how bad the war was going for us, we never believed it. It did not matter how H.V. Kaltenborn spread doom and gloom or how Gabriel Heatter poured it on night after night on every radio in America. They told us we might be beaten, that we might lose the war. While we were aware that there were spies here in our country and people who would betray us, we did not know what one of those people would look like. When we thought about it, naturally we thought they would look like monsters.

Little did we know that at that time they looked just like anyone else and that they were already amongst us as spies and traitors! We had them right there on our County Line Road. In fact, our County Line Road was just freshly graveled by the biggest bunch of traitors of all. The reason they went undetected by anyone as of yet was that only a very few of these new Zionists actually knew that their leaders' stated plans were a cover for their real mission, to divide this country by stuffing the ballot box. They were going to bring the full might of the vote of their membership, and they could do it if there were many, many hundreds of thousands of members voting as instructed.

And those hordes of members *would* vote as instructed, for they marched to their leaders' cadence. These zealots were playing for all the marbles. They had a seemingly unlimited source of finances and an additional supply of money, the dirtiest kind, straight from the extermination ovens all over Poland, Holland, France, Czechoslovakia and Germany itself. They had the money. They just needed the votes, and damn, if they did not almost pull it off.

It was closer than anyone knew.   As fate would have it, only one man could stop this steamroller, and he was still considered by them to be a trusted conspirator, in league with them. All he had was an overpowering need to rid himself of this stench. He was going to put it all on the line. If this stranger claiming to be his long-lost brother had told him the truth, he had to be careful here, then this was a sign from above. It was more than he could have asked for. Not that any man would rejoice over the news of the death of his family, even though he had not seen them in over ten years.

He knew, as only a man in his position could know, that therein lay the answer as to how he could start his campaign to give those monsters the shock of their lives. He would have to move carefully, however, and careful he was.

The fair was in its second day when us kids, twelve and up to fourteen, were asked if we would like to earn some money by picking up trash and such around the fairgrounds, with our parents' permission, of course. We could use our cotton sacks to put the trash into, and while all the parents agreed, most wanted their children to stay up close to the front where they could be seen.

We only were expected to work at this for an hour each day at most, for which we would get paid twenty-five cents each – each day. You can bet that we did a good job. The first day there was a hitch. The second day it seemed all the parents were insistent that their little darlings not, as they said, "drift off" and only stay in the area closest to the front of the fairgrounds.

So that area was receiving a lot of attention, while other places were showing a need of better policing. Mr. Denny put Morley to work cleaning up this much larger area, and Morley asked me if I wanted to help. I said I would have to ask my Dad – we had all planned to go to the fair the last day – and he said there were plenty of chores for me to do around our place. Well, it was not ours, but it is where we lived.

Dad did not know that I had already been to the fair the first day that it opened. My uncle had not told him. Dad decided that he would let me go down and work a while after dark, if I got my chores finished before too late. That was how we talked in those days. "Not too late" referred not to an hour, but more a feeling that it was either too late or not, especially at night. That was assuming, of course, that Mother agreed, which she did not always do.

I got the wood chopped, carried inside and stacked behind the kitchen stove. I got the water pumped for our mules and both the mules and the cows fed. I milked Old Bossy and had it all finished.

I was just settling down with the family to supper. The battery was up, so we had The Amos and Andy Show on the radio, and the program had only just begun when the announcer broke in with an important message.

Now to really understand the alarming effect that this

news bulletin had on us, you have to remember that our country was at war and that quite a lot of us living out there on that County Line had the jitters.

"A German submarine," the announcer said, "has been spotted leaving the Mississippi River, where it empties into the Gulf of Mexico. It is believed that this sub is the same one reported seen as far up the Great River as Cape Girardeau, Missouri. Three German aliens have been detained, all having been put ashore by the captain of the sub. It is suspected that there are several others who as yet have not been brought into custody. They are thought to be armed and dangerous."

That was very unsettling to hear. Cape Girardeau was only about sixty miles from where we lived. What he said as he was winding up his breaking news really put the chill on us. He said they were suspected to be trying to reach safe haven somewhere in Missouri. Everyone in Southeast Missouri, up and down the Mississippi, from New Orleans to Cape Girardeau was to be on the alert. Those foreign agents carried the means to alter their appearance and might appear to be laborers, dock workers or longshoremen.

The men that had been apprehended, it turned out, had crudely drawn maps found on them, showing what was to be the outline of a road that separates the counties of Dunlin and Pemberscott in Southeast Missouri. At the time, the authorities did not know the significance, but the FBI had been alerted.

This left us in stunned silence. At that moment came a

pounding at our back door. Dad grabbed his rifle, a lever-action hex barrel forty-four Winchester, and motioned us to be quiet. He approached the back door with the gun cocked and ready to kill, just as once again the banging resounded on the door. We were all scared until we heard the unmistakable voice of none other than Morley Mitchell.

"You ready, Bobby Snow?"

I must say that we all felt a great relief at that. We had feared the banging on our back door could only be those Germans. We all quickly regained our composure, and when Dad opened the door, the slightly off-center Morley stood there. Dad told him to come on in.

"Bobby's about ready," Dad said. He should have received an award for acting. Morley Mitchell was never aware that only a moment before he was less than a second away from Eternity. "He just needs to finish his supper." Morley came in and saw Dad's gun leaning by the door. "You all too? I can't say I blame you. How did you hear about it?"

Morley was referring to something of great concern to him, which at the time we knew nothing about. Morley got to explaining. He said that his dad's brother had come to stay with them – a strange man, that one – "Have you seen him?" Before Dad could answer, he continued on, saying he had overheard his uncle tell his dad that there was going to be someone slipping into this country from Germany. They would be coming after him, to kill him – that is, the uncle – and again before

Dad could reply he said that last night after his dad blew out the light, they were talking. It was late and they had just gotten back from the fair for the night.

"They thought everyone was asleep," Morley said. "I heard him tell Dad something that I couldn't quite make out. But I did hear him say that they may already be here. He said they couldn't let him live because he knew too much."

It was then that I realized Dad was not going to tell Morley about the news we had just heard on the radio. I suppose it was because he did not know how Morley would act if he became alarmed. I noticed that Morley was calm, especially inasmuch as he had just told us what he heard his uncle say to his dad.

"Uncle asked Dad not to tell anyone down at the fair, and I'm pretty sure he didn't," Morley continued. "But I overheard it and I'm pretty worried. I just had to tell someone, and you Wiltshires have always been straight up with us, so I thought I could trust you." Morley looked at me. "If you don't want to work cleaning up tonight, it's alright."

Then the boy who never ceased to surprise us said, as if reading our minds, "Dad and his brother sure do need some help. They're both pretty concerned. I know they are, even though they both act like they ain't. Even Mother noticed they are worried about something, but she doesn't know what. It would be good if Dad had someone to help him keep an eye on things."

With that, Morley said he should be going and asked if I would be joining him.

"I think it's best if we call it off for tonight," Dad said. "Get a good night's sleep, and we'll see how things are tomorrow. But I have a feeling your Mother, Dad, and Uncle are going to be alright, Morley."

As Morley left, he said, "I know they will if I have anything to do with it."

When he said that, I seemed to notice a display of maturity come over Morley as he stepped out into the dark of the frosty, late October evening. He was gone, but we did not know where. We heard him talk to Myrt, and they trotted off into the night.

Well, that just about tore it for us. We were wondering what Morley could have been talking about. What kind of trouble could his uncle be in, anyway?

Then Mother said, "Now Clyde, do not go getting us involved. It's none of our affair." Dad finally asked if we thought Morley was telling the truth. I spoke up and said that I've known him to be many a thing, but not a liar. My uncle, who lived with us, put in his opinion to back me up, wondering why Morley would have reason to construct such a lie.

"There's got to be something to it alright," my uncle said. "But what? Surely not to do with the news we just heard about."

"I don't know," Dad said. "I don't think there could be a connection."

"I don't reckon so either," Uncle said. "It won't hurt to kind of keep an eye on things, though." "I suppose not," Dad said.

I knew what my uncle meant. Mr. Denny and his brother had just become the luckiest two men in that neck of the woods because Dad and Uncle were, as they said, going to keep an eye on things.

They could do this as well as anyone. They were both men of their word and could not be deterred in their resolve. Once they made up their mind to do something, that something would be done. It was also good to know that they were both outstanding shots, if it came down to needing to use firearms. Dad assured Mother that it would never come to that.

They were just going to keep an eye out for strangers. Under the circumstances, with the fair and all, that would not be easy. Dad said that we should all be doing that anyway, and Uncle was sure that after the news we had heard, this would certainly be on everyone's mind.

Even with all this assurance about no gunplay, I noticed both Dad and Uncle casting their eyes on their trusty Winchesters above the door when they thought Mother was not looking. I know Mother saw them too. Better than anyone, Mother knew this was more serious than we dared suspect. Mrs. Mitchell had come by to visit Mother and had gotten a load off her mind, it seemed.

She talked to Mother about her fears of the danger Mr. Denny was in. He had finally told her about what he was doing the last few years, and in doing so, she became near inconsolable.

Mrs. Mitchell had asked Mother not to speak of it to anyone, but Mother felt Dad should know. She was just going to tell him at supper. When all the rest happened, she decided this would not be the best time, so she waited until Dad and Uncle came back into the house. The two of them sat outside on the front porch having a roll-your-own Prince Albert tobacco cigarette and talking. There was a lot to talk about, but there was going to be a whole lot more.

Mother didn't seem to know where she was going to begin. She was probably thinking to herself that all the Mitchell Family had been up to see us except Mr. Denny himself when Mr. Denny Mitchell pulled up in his truck. "Evening, Clyde – Walker. Glad to see you're up. If you've got a minute, there's something I need to tell you."

Dad told him sure, to come on up. When Mother heard company on the porch, she opened the door and asked Dad if they would like some coffee. She indicated the truck, where another person waited.

"Is that your brother?" Dad asked Mr. Denny. "Have him come up and have some coffee with us."

For the first time, we got to know Mr. Timothy O'Mitchelers. Mr. Denny had shortened his last name to

Mitchell.

There on the porch, over coffee, Mr. Denny Mitchell and his brother took Dad and Uncle into their confidence. They told us things we could not believe, that we did not want to believe, that we were afraid to believe. But it was true.

Dad was silent for what seemed a very long time, as was Uncle. It was so quiet there on the porch, I could almost hear the frost forming. Finally, the silence was broken by the sound of an approaching car. It stopped down a ways from our house. Now, out there on a frosty night sound carries a long way. We heard the car stop, but we did not see any headlights. We thought, why would anyone be driving without their headlights on?

We could see straight down the County Line, and we tried to figure out whose place it had stopped at. Then we figured it was probably someone lost or maybe broken down. We allowed as how they were at least a quarter mile down the road or more – then we did not think any more about it. It was not more than ten minutes before we heard the thing start up again, but still no lights were to be seen. It sounded like they were turning around, then we saw some brake lights, heard whoever it was shift out of low into second, then into high and speed away.

After several minutes, the sound of the engine could no longer be heard. Whoever had turned around there was now long gone, and we all wondered who it might have been. We thought it a little strange and of course we felt like maybe we should move back into the house. The reason given was that it was a little chilly and starting to get late.

Mr. Denny and his brother Timothy said they had to be going. There was a forced effort to assure one and all that things would work out, not to worry. Mr. Denny said there would be horseracing down at the fair tomorrow and told us the track was ready. He already covered two hundred bets and he said tomorrow he was going to enter Bob Tail and Fleet Foot. He also said the quarter horses would be racing Saturday and that would really be something to see.

Then he laughed and remarked, "Myrtle is a quarter horse, did you know that, Bobby?" "Really?" I asked. "Is she going to run?" "Oh, well, I hadn't planned on it. She could probably make a good showing if I had someone run her though. Blind, or near blind, like the old girl is, she has a great heart." He looked at me. "You remember. You rode her that day to get Old Doc. I never did get a chance to ask you how you and her were able to make a long run like you did as fast as you did. Well, like I told you, she has a great heart."

Mr. Denny laughed and showed a little bit of embarrassment. "Yeah, if I let her, but no. I don't think so. But if I would, she would probably put on a show." He turned his attention back to Dad and Uncle. "Come Saturday, our County Line will have her race, alright, but of a kind that one can only pray they will never see again."

At this point, Mr. Denny and his brother were leaving, so we had no way of knowing anything about what awaited us come Saturday.

"I figure," Mr. Denny said, "we better get some rest. Tomorrow should prove to be a big day. Are you ready Timothy?" Then all said goodbye, and they left.

It was a strange night for sure. Dad and Uncle said they could not see any way for Mr. Denny and his brother to handle this terrible situation unless they had some help. With all this danger they were facing I so wanted someone to tell me it was not happening. It seemed unreal.

Ch. 17: The Klan Gathers

In spite of everything, there was a fair that had to open tomorrow – which in two hours would be today – by eleven o'clock. There was so much to do! We all agreed that this must not spill over onto the unsuspecting people coming to our fair. Not one of us, I am sure, could possibly have foreseen what tomorrow would bring.

The first thing I remember of the day was waking to find that Dad and Uncle had left last night, just after I went to sleep. Mother knew about it but would not say where they went. I found out later that they went walking and ended up in Mr. Denny's barn loft.

There they kept an eye out for anyone coming from any direction who might approach the Mitchell house. It seemed they were not up there long before they once again heard the sound of a car engine.

They listened as it slowed to turn off onto our road. This time, however, there was not only the sound of the Model A Ford engine, but others as well, all running close together. They went right on by the Mitchell house, heading, it seemed, toward Gobler.

Then suddenly they stopped, and after about ten minutes or so, they began to turn around and come back. They stopped about a hundred feet or more down from the Mitchell place. There were ten or more vehicles and they had all killed their engines and coasted to a quiet stop on the side of the road, one behind the other. Dad and Uncle watched them as they began to work, putting together several poles, and tying them together to form the shape of a cross.

The Klan had gathered!

As it turned out, there were to be three crosses made in all, if they had gotten them all finished. But a very shadowy figure could just barely be seen creeping up to the last vehicle. It was an old truck with a canvas covering the bed. While these "good citizens" were occupied with their work, this old truck suddenly burst into flames.

When those dullards finally realized what was happening, everyone rushed back to try to beat out the flames on the truck. In doing so, two or more of the misguided fools found the sheets they were wearing had caught fire. While they were busily trying to shed their flaming robes and beat out the inferno that was consuming the bed of the truck, no one saw the limping figure hastily making its way out in the dark, just out of sight up to the lead car, where it suddenly was on fire as well.

As you might imagine, these fools began scurrying about and, not being able to see well as was their plight in those hoods, ran directly into each other. They did not know what to expect next and were so scared that some could be heard screaming for the Illustrious Wizard. While he had accompanied them, he had wisely chosen to stay back down the road, which he probably chose to do for flight reasons. When everything began to go wrong suddenly, they heard his car leaving the scene as it tore off into the night. It seemed the Wizard could be heard winding out that thirty-eight Chevrolet, running like the coward he was. Even though he raced away with his lights on, he wrecked anyway trying to brake to make the turn off the dirt road and onto the main road heading to Kennett. He wrapped his car around a road culvert. He would live, but I am afraid that he lost his lofty position as Wizard, for he had waffled.

What a shame.

Well, with all of this secretive business going awry, it seemed the good members of the Brotherhood had to leave the car where it burned. They did, however, manage to get the truck fire beat out; while it would start, one of the cars would not, so they were forced to leave it, along with the burnt-out car. They made a hasty retreat, leaving behind those burnt and badly scorched sheets, three crosses, one unfinished, as well as two strands of bailing wire used for tying the crosses together.

They also left some burlap sacks to wrap those crosses with and two tins of coal oil. Then, of course, there were the two cars left sitting on the side of our newly graveled County Line Road. One was only a burned-out husk, still showing wraiths of smoke by late the following morning.

The other was still there sitting with both doors wide open, which was a real cause for curiosity because they were still there as people came by the scene on their way to the fair the next morning. Everyone had an opinion as to what it was all about, and everything could be explained away – except for those crosses.

Ch. 18: Mr. Skinner: "Who done it?"

Then there was Mr. Barlow Skinner.

As word got around, he began all over again asking if people saw who done it. It is how it always is when these things happen, only this time someone did see it, from their lofty perch in the barn loft.

Even though it was dark, they could make out to their own satisfaction, thanks to the full moon and the blaze once that old truck burst into flame. For a brief moment who done it could be plainly made out.

I know that Dad, Uncle and I were all saying "good show!" None of us would ever give it away for, after all, I was not there and no one knew that Dad and Uncle were there. They were just keeping an eye on things, as they said, and no one could do better than the two of them.

How lucky to have friends like my dad and uncle were to Mr. Denny Mitchell. For that matter, to many people, me included. They were my uncle and father, but I counted them as friend also. How lucky could one be? Well, Mr. Denny would know soon.

My father and uncle had decided to take upon themselves the safety of Mr. Denny Mitchell and his family. In the case of the Wiltshire family, chivalry was not dead, not in 1942.

Now poor Barlow Skinner was the victim of cruelty at the hands of whoever it was that almost burnt him alive. It went far beyond that, for he was soon being referred to as that dummy who hangs around out on the County Line. So it was that several of the business owners, who were also Klansmen, when they would see Barlow come around would get their kicks by making light of him. He always seemed to them not to be aware of just how cruel they were to him.

Thinking him simple minded, they would talk freely, as if he were not even there. He came to know of their plans to pay a call, as they laughingly said, out to that uppity Denny Mitchell's house on what was for them an ill-fated night. They did not know just yet what happened, but Barlow Skinner knew, for that is the very reason he had made plans.

He went to some trouble to be ready for them when they finally got out there. He had been hiding behind a corrugated grain silo that still had what looked like a piece of tan khaki cloth hanging on it. He did not know that he had been seen, but neither did Dad and Uncle know they had been seen also. You might say that without any of them being aware, they actually seemed to be seeing quite a bit of each other that night.

It seemed it was a very busy night at the Mitchell place. I am sure that stranger things had happened before, and stranger things would happen still out on our County Line Road before all of this would be over.

Now Morley, it seemed, had spent the night at Gobler.

He was still there when his dad and uncle arrived to get the fair ready for opening. There were as many as ten mobile homes and as many horse trailers parked there at Gobler, where the owners planned to stay for the length of the fair. They had brought along certain comforts of home, like folding chairs and barbeque pits, small tables, and big umbrellas that mounted onto the small tables. They looked to be enjoying a camping trip, Morley had said. He was going to make sure that everything was all right.

That was what he had said, anyway. What he did not say was that he had gone to the track to put Myrt through some trial runs, in the dark, mind you. Morley was not afraid of the dark, as he should have been, especially where he was. He did not think anyone would hear him, but several of the campers did and came out to see what was going on. They got to see the old girl run and they would put the watch on her, and several found it hard to believe that the clock was accurate. They wondered could the old girl really clock that kind of time. If they were right, well, it beat anything they had ever seen, and they were people who knew about horses.

Morley was very happy about that, and he was smiling when he put her up after rubbing her down real good. He fed her well, oats and a little barley, given to him by the people who had watched Myrt run. They both got a little sleep. Morley slept by Myrt until he woke up. She seemed to be restless and nudged him. He thought it was her way of showing her affection to him for feeding her so well.

But no, it wasn't that at all. It was something else. As he rubbed the sleep from his eyes, he noticed there was a flickering light coming from inside a window in the front of his dad's large corrugated steel building. It was only there for a second. As he waited and watched, he did not see it again. .

He began to wonder if he had really seen it to begin with. He shrugged it off and got onto Myrt for waking him up. Then he tried to drop off back to sleep. It did not come easy, and as he was just about to fall asleep, he lunged up into a setting position as if he had been rudely shaken awake.

He was just in time to hear people talking, at least two men. He could not make out a thing they were saying. They were coming his way, and because they were not expecting anyone to be there in the dark, they did not see him in the deep shadows of the trees.

There was no moon in sight. They walked right by him, and Morley could smell whiskey. They sounded like they had been drinking, even though he could not understand a word they were saying. He watched them fade into the night, heading in the direction of the road leading away from Gobler. Then he heard what he believed to be a truck stopping. He figured they got in it, and then they were gone.

Then, if you can believe it, Morley said he went back to sleep.

Once again, I had the feeling that Morley just was not

right in the head, but this was, after all, Morley Mitchell we are talking about, and I think it is safe to say that it happened just as he said. He had seen at least two of the saboteurs we were warned about on the radio, and it was just as his uncle had said: they were already there.

As Morley had not heard the broadcast, he had no way of knowing that he had just escaped disaster for the second time, all in less than five hours.

Evidence of God, if I ever saw it.

He did not tell his dad or uncle about Myrt's unusual actions. Neither did he tell them about the light he thought he saw coming from inside the store. Worse yet, he did not mention anything about the two men who came by him, speaking in a strange language early that morning.

He said nothing at all until his dad was just about to unlock the huge front door. He finally mentioned the light he saw, and his dad was so shocked that it caused him to drop the keys.

"Don't open that door," his Uncle Timothy shouted. "Everyone get away from here. That door may be wired with explosives."

We all ran back and his uncle backed off ever farther, looking at the top of the building.
"Denny, your gable window is open," Uncle Timothy said.

Three gables were built into the roof, one in the front, one in the center and one near the back. Uncle Timothy said that it looked like someone might have broken in the night before.

"Oh yeah, I forgot to tell you," Morley said. "I saw two men early this morning. They were talking in a funny language."

Uncle Timothy went looking for a ladder. Denny told him where to find it and he put it up against the building. He climbed up to the top and through the window, dropping down inside. He yelled for Denny to send up his knife, and Mr. Denny Mitchell did as he was asked, pitching it through the open window.

"Everyone get back," Uncle Timothy yelled from inside. "This door is rigged to blow up when its opened."

Mr. Denny and Morley both backed off quite a way. So far, no one had come up, but that could change at any moment. From the building came nothing but silence. Denny and Morley were almost afraid to breathe.

After what seemed like forever, the front door opened and Uncle Timothy came out with a strange device in his hand. It looked to be the size of a large Cracker Jack box with wires trailing out behind.

Uncle Timothy was very tense. He took off his jacket and quickly wrapped the thing, saying, "I got it. I checked and didn't find any more but Denny, we've got company.

"It was a close call, and I don't know if we'll be as lucky next time, but –" Uncle Timothy paused. "Whoever put this here will be expecting an explosion. We should keep this thing out of sight and wait. Maybe we can get it back to them and then we'll give them their explosion."

"How did you know what to do?" Morley asked his uncle. "Laddie, I was a specialist in the IRA, handling explosive ordinance."

Morley did not know what that meant, but his dad did. Then Uncle Timothy said, "I know how to blow things up. That's what they want, then that's what I'll try and give 'em, but first we've got to learn for sure just who we're dealing with. For now it's show time and there is a fair to be enjoyed so Denny, what say we open this one up and let the games begin?"

Uncle Timothy turned to Morley. "Find us some of those bells, and let's get things started." Before long, Morley was back with several bells, and the three of them began joyously ringing them. The clangs and rings pealed forth through the cool morning air and with that, Mr. Denny declared the fair officially open for the third day.

Ch. 19: A Racehorse Falls Over Dead

That day turned out to be an overwhelming success. The people came to have a good time, none the wiser about anything. The booths all did a lively business. Judges judged many recipes and winners were declared, blue ribbons awarded while second and third place took the red and yellow.

Boys chased greased pigs and in general made fools of themselves, which was why they did it to begin with. Hammers were thrown, poles were tossed, footraces were held, and broad jumps took place. Some won, some lost, and the young all had a real good time. Last but not least came the horses. For the very first time they were turned loose to battle it out on the three-mile long regulation-sized racetrack.

One horse died during first race. He tripped because of his rider taking him off track for a shortcut. The rider was thrown when the horse shied up, having seen what the rider said was "Something terrible, something awful."

He was talking gibberish about how it just rose up out of the swamp. We all thought, sure.

Cheaters always tell such lies.

Someone pointed out that we should consider the nature of his injuries and those of the horse, which was still alive at this point. Since horse and rider were disqualified for leaving the track, he stammered and stuttered, saying he did. not give a hoot. He appeared frightened, and before he could be treated at the first aid tent, he left the fairgrounds.

Someone said he was helped away by two men whose talk sounded strange. He was last seen being put into a car by those two men and spirited away. He was gone before he could be questioned about what he really saw in the swamp.

Most of us figured he just saw the last of one of the huge black bears. They were not grizzly, but about as large as one. Some swore they were still out there in the swamp.

What little he said, though, no one could make much sense of. Some of the first ones to reach him when he came dragging back said he smelled like rotten cabbage. While this was being discussed, the woman who owned the horse came running up to Mr. Denny, screaming that her horse had just fallen over dead.

She said when he breathed out his last, his breath smelled like rotten vegetation, and now she was feeling sick. She wanted to know what was happening. Then she went into convulsions and died. Another person who had been there when the horse died became ill as well and was taken to lie on a cot.

Everyone wondered what was going on. Then an ancient old-timer who had served in World War I said that it looked like they may have been overcome by gas of some sort. He had seen it once before, in France, when the Germans attacked with gas that killed those that breathed it, just like the woman.

This went over like a lead balloon. Everyone who heard this, there were about a dozen, were afraid to breathe, and I cannot say that I blame them. This began serious face watching of each other, but there was no panic. After a few minutes when no one else seemed affected, the tension backed off some.

The old veteran said, "Nope, I don't think this is the same thing. No rash around her lips or neck that I can see. Would be if it were the gas they used in the Big War. Nope, definitely not the same."

Then Mr. Denny declared that he believed it to be swamp gas. He remembered the two old hermits he bought the land from mentioning finding game dead for no apparent reason. It was always deep in the heart of the swamp. Back then, he had suspected it, but since there had been no signs, had more or less forgotten about it.

That was what he told the people that were gathered. When the woman arrived, a man had run to get him, Mr. Denny was naturally overcome with personal guilt over her death. Her husband was very sad and overcome with emotion, but he was able to declare that she had been in very bad health, and he had expected that this might happen. He said that when her horse had died so suddenly, he thought it was just too much for her and she suffered a heart attack. Her heart had been very weak for a long time, and that idiot son of hers had probably ridden the horse to death.

As the husband mourned, he said that he had told her she should not enter him into the endurance race. He was not trained for such a run. She insisted, so he gave in to her as he always had.

"I suppose I should not fault Albert," he said, referring to the man riding the horse. "Even though we knew him sometimes to be a little unstable, I knew that at one time he had been a very good rider, good enough to have ridden once on the same track as great horses like Sea Biscuit and Dan Patch. Then a few years back he had a bad fall. We thought he had recovered his balance enough to enter the competition again and hoped this would be the thing he needed to rebuild his confidence. He could get his life straightened out.

 "It would have done so much for my wife too. He was her son by her first marriage. He and his two brothers came all the way down from Old German Town in Chicago and bet heavy on him. They were so anxious to see him ride again, but now he's disgraced us all by cheating."

Her husband wiped a few tears away before he continued. "Well, at least she did not know he cheated, because that would have killed her for sure."

All that the man was saying sounded strange, being said at just this time. Then the man lying on the cot spoke up.

"I hope you don't mind," the man said. "I've been lying

here listening to you while expecting to die myself. It just dawned on me if your old lady died of a heart attack and that damn fool of a son rode that nag to death, then I ain't lying here dying like I thought I was, am I? There wasn't any poison gas at all."

He got up and asked where to go puke. "I think the only thing wrong with me is I ate some of Mrs. Peabody's sorghum, carrot, allspice Dutch apple pie. I bought her pie, so she came right over there and watched me finally have some to eat. Someone said it was customary and now I'm sick. I gotta go. Sorry about your wife's horse."

With that, he ran out of the tent looking for a place to put Mrs. Peabody's god-awful pie, not fit for human consumption, where it would not hurt anyone, if there were such a place. He thought it would probably kill a tree, but he let it go. As he said to himself, better a tree than me. *What a relief,* he thought, but he did not see Mrs. Peabody walking up.

We will cut away, though, as we cannot help this poor fellow anyhow.

We had big troubles of our own. We had narrowly averted what would have been a real disaster, and it was beginning to be just one narrow escape after another. We could not see how it could get any worse, but of course, it did.

For now, however, the fair went on. Mr. Denny first helped the man to make arrangements for his late wife. They moved her to a funeral home in Kennett. Then he got upon that little cart and personally dragged the horse out into the timber and graded out a gravesite so they would have a place to bury the horse. It would be without much ceremony, but a burial just the same.

Mr. Denny did all this to help the man who by then had left with the hearse carrying his dead wife to Kennett. Mr. Denny buried the horse deep so that wild animals would not get at him.

Overall, it was an unusual day at our County Fair. No one could have predicted such a day as this. We still had two more days of fair, fun, frivolity and festivity left. That was assuming, of course, that our central characters could manage to stay alive.

Now Dad and Uncle Walker were good friends with a fellow who ran the local pool hall, called Shields, in Kennett. It just happened to be the only pool hall with regulation-size tables that did not suffer from what regulars called "flat cushions." This was where Uncle would come face to face with the Nazis who came looking for Mr. Denny Mitchell. Instead, they met Uncle.

Uncle did not know who they were at first. They looked about like anyone else in there on a Saturday morning. It seemed our would-be killers were in need of diversion. These men were bold and arrogant but good with a stick, a pool stick that is. Thinking they were safe and no one would know who they were, they ventured forth to play some pool. Since the only decent pool hall around was Shields, this was where they ended up, playing on a table next to the one Uncle was playing on.

They knocked their brake ball off the table and it came to a stop against the wall next to where Uncle was chalking up and waiting for a game with Tommy, the owner. He retrieved their ball and was in the process of returning it to them. Now Uncle was always looking for new faces, someone he might get up a game of pool with, a friendly game perhaps.

The best way to do this was to seem clumsy in some manner. So, as he returned the ball to the man doing the break, Uncle pitched the ball up as he was carrying it, made as if to try to catch it, and missed. He knocked the ball across the room and, showing signs of embarrassment, scurried after it.

Uncle noticed the men were laughing at him. He handed the ball back to one of the fellows. The man spoke some English with a little difficulty and asked if he would like to play some pool. Then he turned to his companions, laughed and explained in German that he had found a pigeon.

Uncle understood what was implied. The man turned back to him with a derisive smile still on his face and said, "You want to play, *ja*?"

"I'll play," Uncle replied. "But not for much money."

The German turned to his fellows, told them he was going to play this hayseed and asked how much money they had. They pooled their money, but not their Marks as he was just American, and it looked like they had about twenty dollars or so. Uncle protested, saying it was too much. He only had ten, and really just wanted to play for fun.

"*Ja, ja,*" the fellow responded. "We play just for fun. We play twenty dollars for your ten dollars, and you can break the balls."

Uncle studied them for a moment or two and then counted out his own money. It came to ten dollars and some change. Then he decided against playing for money. He returned to his table and proceeded to spin the break ball with his fingers, seeming to be completely content with doing this. All the while, the three disappointed Germans continued to watch Uncle, completely satisfied that this rube was an easy mark that they just could not justify letting off the hook. They decided to up the ante and approached Uncle again. This time they almost demanded that he play with them, allowing as how he had insulted them and when he insulted them, he insulted Germany.

Now Uncle had to play or fight.

Uncle said, almost scared like, that he did not want to play them, but he would if they would sweeten the deal. After all, it was clear they could beat him easily enough. If they would put up everything they had, what was in their pockets, their Marks, their rings and knives, guns too, against his almost eleven dollars –

"It's an uneven bet," Uncle said. "But you've put this on

a personal basis. It comes down to an American country dirt farmer, me, against a boorish big mouth German backed up by two flunkies, namely you three.

"I'll bet you because if I should beat you, well the best I could say was that I only beat several third rate Nazis. Oh yes, I know who you are, but don't let that fact make you nervous. We've got a bet. So get your money and valuables on the table. Here's mine." Uncle laid down his money. "We'll just let Tommy hold everything. Now either put up, or shut up."

The idea that they may have misjudged their mark must have slowly been crossing their minds.

"You rack 'em and I'll break 'em," Uncle said.
The three Germans had a brief meeting at the end of the table, totally upset as the one who spoke English explained it all to them. He really did not know, but his was better than an educated guess. They were exactly who Uncle had figured them for being. They broke and ran out of the place, leaving behind the collateral they were going to use to cover the sucker bet.

Neither Tommy nor Uncle followed them. They really had no reason to do so, and the Sheriff was preoccupied over in the next county, being entertained by Miss Taffy out on her veranda, where she served him sweets of one kind or another along with oh so smooth libations. That was where he was to be found every second Saturday because Miss Taffy was looking to be married, and it was our city police chief of Kennett who was targeted to be the lucky man.

Well, I heard that story differently. Looking back on it, I'm not sure what I thought at the time about Taffy and the Sheriff in my 10-year-old head, probably didn't give it much thought at all. But I do vaguely remember something about the Sheriff being seen out on that veranda in some sort of pink outfit, which, I need not tell you, didn't sound like *our* Sheriff at all. Before I venture further, I must say that it was not Miss Taffy that was wearing the pink outfit. It was the Sheriff himself, according to the selfsame person who says he saw him in the get-up.

The story goes that the Sheriff, who was a lean and lanky sort, not unlike John Wayne in his looks and his demeanor, which could and did put the fear of God in anyone bent on a bad deed and happening to cross his path while perpetratin' it, had a softer side which Miss Taffy enjoyed helpin' him indulge on a quiet afternoon.

And that softer side had to do with wearing a giant set of pink pyjamas complete with feet… like a child's set of pajamas might have, and a matching pink hat with bunny ears. Where he got a set of pink PJs quite like that in his size was a mystery until I saw the adult Halloween costume collection in the Sears Roebuck catalog from a couple of years later. And there it was in all its pink perfection.

Now if I hadn't known the person who told this story I wouldn't have believed it for the moon. But, well, that person was pretty trustworthy, so I say if that's what it takes to get you stirred up enough to go out and hunt down the bad guys, why, so what. And knowing Miss

Taffy had a good-size funny bone, I expect that giant pink bunny jimjam outfit had something to do with a joke known only to the two of them.

But getting back to our story, since our Sheriff was indisposed and unavailable, those three Germans got away clean – for the time being. It would not last long.

One can only wonder what they did between that day in the pool hall and their final curtain that would come down for them in little more than two days. Time was running out fast. These men fancied themselves superior to my uncle, the dirt farmer; they had called him a *Schweinebüttel*. It was a big insult, meaning literally, "pig policeman," "one who lived with and sold pigs for a living."

They also believed themselves to be smarter than Americans. Uncle must have posed quite the dilemma to them, then. He probably made them second-guess themselves about who else might know about them.

Could just anyone know what they were up to?

It just proved once again that the best laid plans of mice and men have a way of going astray. It seems there is another saying that would certainly apply. If you handle dynamite – well, I do not recall the whole thing but eventually, you can expect it to go Boom!

That is what would come to pass. These three men would surely die, but sad to say we would never really know for sure just who they were. Once my tale is complete, however, you are free to speculate, and I thank you if you do.

Ch. 20: The German Blacksmith Visits

Just outside of Kennett, a man by the name of Kirk Sturgeon owned and operated the only blacksmith shop for miles around. He was an old German fellow, a stern man who worked hard for very little money, mind you. He had a red beard and reddish hair with lots of gray in it. He was unkempt, that is a bit wild to look at. When he held that heavy hammer in his hand, he looked fearsome.

He was a giant of a man and short tempered. At times, he would speak German and would appear exasperated when one would not understand him. He wore an old heavy leather apron with many signs of burning sparks from his forge. His anvil would come to life as he went about turning out the sharpest plow shears a farmer could ask for.

Now old man Sturgeon was gruff and did not suffer fools lightly. Still, he had a following that kept him busy. People passing by on the road would just wave or honk and if they had no business with Sturgeon would keep on going. He would just wave that huge hammer above his head and never look up. If you pulled into his place of business, such as it was, it was customary to stand by your vehicle, watch, and listen as he reduced whatever he was working on to perfection.

It could well be three or four minutes before he would raise that huge head of his, and then you were treated to his full attention. It was then that you noticed that he had bright blue eyes, blistered arms, cracked lips, and very few teeth. Before he would speak to you, you could not help but be impressed by the total interest he was always showing towards the particulars of the job he was working on as well as the banging, clanging rhythm. He was always pounding away with his different hammers, depending on what was required for the work at the time.

There was something about the smell of that forge, the hot metal he worked with, and the dirt floor that he kept slightly damp. It just seemed to invite the results that you could only attain from mingling the odor of a hardworking man with those of his environment, as was with the case of Kennett's only blacksmith, Mr. Kirk Sturgeon.

My father and uncle, I am only too happy to say, were very good friends with him.

They were such good friends that when we would stop by to bring him our plow shears or whatever we had for sharpening, he would ask us to come round back where he kept some cold beer, sausage he called Knockwurst, and a hogshead of strong yellow cheese. Then he would take that old towel and make as if to tidy up a bit.

He had an old rickety table covered with an even older oilcloth. He would find us something to sit on and we would gather around. With noticeable pride, he would slice pieces of that strong smelling cheese and lay it around the tablecloth for us, proceed to cut us handsome pieces from that string of knockwurst, and set before

Dad and Uncle cold bottles of German beer. He would give us several large crackers as well, and for me a cold Pepsi.

After that, we would all go to town. All this did not take long, but it was a treat and old man Sturgeon would just beam with pleasure, obviously content to be with Dad and Uncle. He would brag about the simple things of life, like that wonderful German sausage, how great the cheese was from the Old Country, and how much better real beer was, straight from Copenhagen.

It was easy to see that in spite of our cultural differences, they all truly enjoyed each other's company. Dad and Uncle were totally accepted by this gruff and lonely man, lonely by choice as Dad and Uncle never treated him as anything other than an American.

Though I think most people did treat him as if he did not belong, not really realizing they were doing so. Old man Sturgeon was never known to be one to visit. He just took care of the needs of the farming community.

One day, after we had done some slight favor for him, I disremember what it was, Mr. Sturgeon sent a neighbor boy to tell our family that we weren't to worry about dinner that night but just to show up at his house at a particular time. So we did.

And don't you know, he had fixed us the fanciest old German-style dinner you could ever hope for – we had him write down the words for each dish, what they meant in English and even a recipe for what he called the *schnitzels*, pork cutlets pounded paper thin, rolled in beaten egg and then in dry breadcrumbs; and then shallow fried in butter in the big iron skillet. Those schnitzels were almost bigger than the plates he put them on, because of all that pounding, but it was the sauce that made the dish. These particular schnitzels were called Jaegerschnitzels (hunter's schnitzel) because you were supposed to be able to find the main ingredients for the sauce out in the woods. Well now, I don't know if I would trust my own judgment or that of any of the family members to know which mushrooms were edible in that neck of the woods and which might kill you, but we just let Mr. Sturgeon make that decision and not one of us fell over dead. To this day I've had a special place in my heart for schnitzel.

When it came to needing his help, he did this for a very fair price. He kept mainly to himself; it would seem that Dad and Uncle were his only trusted friends. It was because they just had that way about them that would draw people towards them. They were, after all, very easy to like.

Therefore, it came as a surprise when Mr. Sturgeon showed up at our humble home, hurt, with dried blood on his head and all over his faded blue work shirt. He came out to our place in Kennett's only taxi. He needed help, he said, he was in serious trouble. It seemed that three strangers showed up at his workshop speaking German and wanting him to put them up for a few days. These visitors had the names and some addresses of certain people here who still had family in Germany. It was felt they could be depended on to provide certain services if the need might present itself. In their case, they had met this farmer, did not know his name, who seemed to spell trouble for them. Because Sturgeon's name was on their list as one who should be contacted, they had come fully expecting to receive assistance in this matter having to do with business of the Third Reich. But no, this was not to be because Sturgeon's loyalties were not with the Nazis.

With the old Germany, yes, but he now had another country that he felt loyal to, this America. He now thought of it as his home. He had good friends here, and he would not betray them or his new country. He told them to get out, at which time they set to work on him with hammer and tongs found right there in his blacksmith shop. Though he was a mighty man, they had struck swiftly, catching him off guard. They were trying to shove his bead into his forge when a customer showed up. They scurried out back and left old man Sturgeon for dead. Once again, they were able to make their getaway. However, their time was running out. Old man Sturgeon did not see who had come up at just the right time, but it was Barney, the one-armed cabdriver.

Barney owned Kennett's only cab company, which at that time amounted to just the one cab. He had only just started his cab business about two months ago, having lost his arm in a hay bailing mishap. He lost it almost to the shoulder. It was especially bad inasmuch as Barney was right-handed. To be able to drive, shift gears, he had appealed to Mr. Sturgeon to make a device whereby he could shift that old Dodge with his right foot.

Sturgeon had made it. It was a strange apparatus to be sure, but Barney could make the gears shift with it. Old Sturgeon had just given it to him, and this night Barney was coming by to take him over to Dalton's for one of his great hamburgers.

Dalton owned and operated Kennett's only hamburger stand, and without a doubt made the best burgers on the Missouri side of the Mighty Mississippi. Oddly enough, Dalton had only one hand. On the other hand, he had lost all but his pointer finger and thumb. Dalton had fed Barney several times when he was first getting started with his taxi business because he was broke. Dalton, being a kindly person, would just say, "Pay me when you get some money, Barney," and Barney would do just that. Barney would throw Dalton business whenever he could.

Barney coming by as he did that night probably saved Kirk Sturgeon's life, for he was beat unconscious. Though Barney had only the one arm, he was able to get this badly injured giant of a man into that old Dodge. Mr. Sturgeon began moaning, "Get me to Clyde's place."

Barney, like everyone else, knew of my father, for he would sometimes in years past work for us. This was, of course, before he had become the transportation tycoon that he was now. He lost his right arm while reaching in to the bailer cavity of an old relic of a hay bailer, left out at our place by the people who owned it, none other than the Great General American Land Company.

Sadly, the plunger got him on its downward stroke, but in any event, during this emergency Barney would have no trouble finding our place because his entire right arm was buried out behind our barn.

Barney was almost beside himself. When he finally got out to our place, he would not leave Sturgeon alone in the cab to come and get help. He was struggling to get him up on the porch, when we, being aware of a commotion, came to the front door to see the two of them collapsed on the porch steps. Barney was calling out for help, and Mr. Sturgeon was moaning like he was dying.

The man was injured badly about the head, and we at first feared he had suffered a broken jaw. It looked like he was now blind in his right eye as well, but even so he was trying to tell Dad something. May God bless his soul. It was a ghastly sight to be sure, but Dad and Mother never wavered.

We got him into the kitchen and laid him on a folding Army cot. I did not believe it could sustain the weight, and though it sagged and creaked quite a bit, it held and Mother went to work tending to him.

We still had some of that wonderful medicine old Doc Spears had given us. We used that to a good purpose. We got him cleaned up and doctored as best we could, and he drifted off to sleep. We asked Barney what had happened, and he did not know much to tell us, except Old Sturgeon had rambled on about the Nazis being here. The three men wanted his help to hide them. When he would not help them, they tried to kill him.

"Did you see them?" Dad asked. Barney said no, they were not there when he arrived. He figured he did not miss them by more than a few seconds, but he went on to say it looked like old Sturgeon put up a good fight. There was lots of blood, mostly on that big wide curved blade; he probably was sharpening it when he was attacked. He was not able to say much more, only that he wanted to come here.

Dad told Barney he should have taken him to Doc Spears. Barney said Sturgeon did not want no Doctor, just wanted to come here. "How is he, Mrs. Wiltshire?" Barney asked Mother. "I don't know," Mother replied. She had tapped open the Kerr lid on a Mason jar full of good rich homemade chicken soup. She said that after he slept a while, she would try to get some down him.

Barney said he did not know just what he had gotten mixed up in, but felt like he had better be getting on back. He asked if we wanted him to send the doctor on out here. Mother said he could if it was not a bother, and he said he would try to get back up with him. Then he left us.

It was with some misgiving that we realized that here we were with a badly injured man, and no way to get any help if he took a turn for the worst.

As we were just sitting there watching Mr. Sturgeon and listening to his labored breathing, a shot knocked out our window in the front room. It liked to scared us out of our wits, and in a flash Dad had his trusty forty-four Winchester off the rack above our front door. At the same time, he waved us all down flat on the floor.

Then we heard the sound of boots on our front porch. The door busted in, and a wild-eyed, torch-wielding maniac burst into our home. Mad as a hornet, Dad shot him.

He did not kill him. He only spun him around, but the man stayed on his feet and went stumbling back through the door. Everything was happening so quickly. Dad tried to put out the fire the man started. He was not able to get off another shot, and the fool made it off the porch and out to the road, but not before almost knocking Uncle down in his desperate dash to get away.

He managed to get into a car that had just driven up, for that very reason it seemed, and was gone into the night. Uncle was just coming up on foot, having only just returned from a walk down to Mr. Denny's house. After the immediate excitement was over, Uncle dropped a bomb, in a manner of speaking.

He told us that this fool that had ran into him, the one who left his blood on Uncle's shirt, was not one of the three seen at the pool hall. That meant that there were at least four of them, and Dad remarked, "Now come morning there won't be four unless the one I just put that bullet in gets some help."

Dad and Uncle figured that these killers had stolen a car – it looked a lot like old Doc's – before or after they had tried to kill Mr. Sturgeon, and had followed Barney out to our place to finish him off. We did not know just why they were so intent on killing old man Sturgeon or for that matter why they had fired only the one shot.

Unless they were themselves surprised when they saw a familiar looking man coming up on them from out of the dark. For whatever reason, they sent this dense individual to execute this dumbest of all acts. For all his efforts, he would only manage to get himself badly shot. He failed in his ill-conceived attempt to terrorize us.

Their entire effort this night, it seemed, would end in failure even more than they could have imagined. They were now out in the open and had made the mistake of getting my dad angry. This in itself was not a good thing, as you can imagine.

However, these bad boys now knew where we all lived. Here we were all under one roof. It was around midnight; we had no car, no telephone, and no way to get any help out here. Our hope was that they would be so busy with the wounded man and trying to get away with having stolen a car, understanding they were in a strange country.

Everything was not so ideal for them either, overall. The worst of it was they could not run the risk of getting their man to a Doctor, for that would tip their hand as to who they were. Thus, we felt that at least for tonight we had battled them to a stalemate.

It was then that Mr. Sturgeon's cot collapsed. He started

trying to get up and could not, so Dad and Uncle helped him stand and assisted him over to the kitchen table. He sat down on a chair and looked in a daze. His one eye was glassy, and we could see that he was disoriented. He was silent, but smelled the chicken soup Mother was heating up. He took a handkerchief from his front pocket and put it up beside the injured eye. By now that eye was as much out of its socket as it was in. He turned his massive head at an angle and looked around, seemingly aware for the first time that he was not alone.

"Mein Gott, do I smell Hühnersuppe?" *My God, do I smell chicken soup?* He asked in a happy voice.

Dad and Uncle shook his hand and patted his back while Mother served up a large helping of Granma Watson's – Mother's mother – hot, rich, healthy, wholesome – made from a German recipe – something you could not buy in any restaurant or store, delicious, soul-restoring, quick healing, mother-knows-best chicken soup.

I got to feed it to him spoonful by spoonful, and boy, we could see his spirit revive. I tell you my people were the greatest. We did not have a dime to spare, it seemed, but we never knew we were poor. There was so much love in our life.

Looking back, I cannot remember a day that I was not happy, but none more so than that particular night when I was allowed to spoon-feed the chicken soup that mother had made to our good friend who had been badly beaten by those Nazi thugs.

Our Mr. Kirk Sturgeon was our very own blacksmith, who I knew to be a very wonderful man. He had needed our help, and by the Eternal, we would help him.

I felt so good, so proud that with all these dangers I could only think, bring 'em on.

Well, speaking of the Eternal, God was about to intervene, for after all we were all running on his timetable whether we knew it or not.

Ch. 21: The European Scene Worsens

Now as I tell this story, I realize that I need to tell you a little more about the overriding forces behind the events taking place in our little part of the world. In those dark and fearful days of 1940 through 1945, well, there was a power play taking place on a global scale in Europe.

Hitler had come to power in Germany and by 1939 had taken complete and total control of the country. He declared himself dictator and began manifesting his unbridled ambition to subdue the entire world. He would do this through war or any other means he deemed necessary – cunning and guile, threats and promises made with the full intent to break them when he felt it expedient.

Of course, force was at the very heart of his manifesto for becoming supreme dictator of the entire world. His plans for accomplishing this first appeared in a book he wrote while in prison for having failed in an earlier attempt to take over the government of Germany. He found himself languishing away in a prison cell for his failure; however, he was not alone. In that very same prison was another fellow who would play a very important part in Hitler's future and his improbable though rapid rise to total dictatorial power.

In that prison was none other than Rudolf Hess. Now there was a perfect example of two kindred spirits meeting in the most unlikely of places. They met at just the right moment in time and what followed would cause the world to moan and despair while the Devil rejoiced and declared, "Look there! Look there! Through these two sick men, I will spread wanton murder and destruction on a scale the world has never seen before."

I am sure that in Satan's camp these two misfits finding each other was truly a cause for rejoicing.

You see, coupled with them was a certain Benito Mussolini, who was already the dictator of Italy. By the time Hitler was sprung from that prison and finally came to power, Mussolini had already formed his own fascist government. Hitler admired Mussolini and his smooth murdering, fascist regime and modeled his own brand of dictatorship after Mussolini's.

With this kind of admiration between the two dictators, what else would they do except join forces with one another. It seemed that – surprise, surprise – Benito had also been harboring ambitions for world domination for quite some time. He knew that he could not do it alone, but now with this new boy on the block by the name of Adolf Hitler, things were beginning to look up for him.

Benito would help his newfound friend with a certain problem he was having – how best to get a toehold in America in a manner whereby he could exercise the most control. His need was to undermine our Democratic process and to control the vote in this country. In this way, he would keep America out of the war they were going to wage.

These two were not too worried about taking over Europe. That was a given, with France being a joke and England being even funnier. In Spain there was a fellow Dictator with a good Latin name of Franco. He could be bought or quickly brought in line, though Spain decided to remain neutral.

No, the only real problem as Hitler and Mussolini saw it was America. Mussolini rightly figured that the best way to control us was to use our own political system against us, by controlling our vote.

Now Mussolini was himself a good Catholic boy at heart. He put a bug in Hitler's ear as to his awareness of a certain rather large religious group here in the Colonies – not the Catholic Church – who he knew from his own agents here just happened to have itchy palms, attentive ears and coveting eyes. He felt they could hold the key to Hitler's dilemma, if they were offered just the right incentive, like sharing in the conquest after the war, in return for using their considerable influence to push the vote against America coming into the War in Europe against them every time it came up on our ballots.

They did indeed strike an agreement, which was accepted rather quickly by all. To Hitler and his ilk, it meant nothing. To this worldwide religious body, however, it meant everything. I should point out that while the Saints and Angels, this is how they preferred to be called, especially the higher mucky-mucks had more than a touch of greed and larceny in their hearts, they were but babes in arms when it came to dealing with the Nazis.

It seems there will never be a shortage of misguided souls who are too willing to buy into every new religion – or better put, cult – that shows up on the doorsteps of society.

They continue to come in many forms, but are always promoted by some clever, long-winded, self-proclaimed Messiah who but for the willingness of so many lambs to offer themselves to be led to the slaughter would quickly fade away.

You see, there is a pool of the pathetic lost these hustlers can always count on: they turn to their followers, and always for their money.

Naturally, in some way there will be a need for them to fork over their money, and on a regular basis at that. It is amazing how that part of their fraud always works to perfection. But alas, there is always going to be the self-described prophet with some hair-brained scheme, the more bizarre the better, just as surely as there will always be the ones drawn to that individual's spiel about how he or she can lead them to the promise land.

These phonies learned a simple but little recognized fact, and they all had the brass to launch their carriers on this simple understanding about people. It is this: if you can get people to accept your premise, it matters not what the discussion is about – though how much better if it is about religion, for then that person is onto a more or less sure thing –then they will naturally buy the bit. It is a show business axiom that goes back to the days of the Caesars. So effective is this gambit that Joseph Goebbels, Hitler's minister of propaganda, started in 1936 with the same idea, just presented in a different manner. The bigger the lie, the more willing people are to accept it and act on it.

Thus, Goebbels was able to turn the non-Jew Germans against the Jews to such an extent that before Hitler was defeated, his murdering machine exterminated some six million Jews as well as others that the Nazis deemed inferior; the Gypsies, the sick, mentally challenged and all political opposition. He spread the humongous lie that these people were enemies of the State and in order for a pure Aryan race of supermen and superwomen to be developed, it was not only permissible but mandatory that all non-Aryans, as well as those who were sick, weak, and crippled, be removed from the new Germany's society. They therefore were no longer entitled to live.

Goebbels sold this as a premise in every media that Germany had at its disposal. Newspapers, newsreels, radio, movies and speeches – ah yes, the speeches – made to the masses spewed forth every filthy lie, all designed to turn the world against the Jews – especially the Jews.

He identified them as the cause of Germany's Great Depression. The Jews were very prosperous and industrious. They were shopkeepers and moneylenders. They owned pawnshops and almost every average German was personally indebted to some Jew during the

Great Depression. Since the Jews were the cause of Germany's desperate economic situation – according to Goebbels' lies – it seemed the perfect solution to imprison them. With their imprisonment, the debt of every Jew's neighbor would be wiped out. The Jew's property would be taken over, and the Jews would be exterminated.

Germany would be better off.

It was the perfect solution if you were a mad dog tyrant like Hitler and his henchmen all certainly were. Had it not been for the horrible murder of all these innocent Jews and other "undesirables", Hitler's plan for world conquest might have worked.

Something so unbelievable, so unspeakable as the wholesale slaughter of millions of innocent human beings, well, it finally began to shock the decent sensibilities of the free, civilized world.

Though the premise was that being a Jew was the problem, decent people could no longer deny the obvious, that we could not just continue to stand by and do nothing while this inhumanity towards the weak and helpless was going on.

It no longer mattered what their premise was, or about these undesirables having to die not only for the betterment of Germany but also for the whole world. They were identified as vermin, rats, filthy, evil and the killers of Christ, none of which was true. At that time, however, Germany thought of itself as both a Protestant and Catholic nation. Laughable as it may seem now, there was then still a score to be settled. It was taught from every pulpit that the Jews had crucified our sweet Lord on the cross. It was not true, the Romans did that foul deed, but because at that time it was a pagan Roman World and a young Church found it expedient not to place the blame on Rome for the execution of our Savior, it was easier and more prudent to blame Jesus' death on the Jews.

That blame became a premise, and it served all the desired purposes and ulterior motives of that age. A fledgling Church was just getting started. Yet even today, more than two thousand years later, every little Johnny Come-Lately is still perpetuating that same gargantuan lie.

It is called crowd-baiting, and they just want to make a name for themselves in the religious arena. Sadly all too often this rubbish is served up by well-established and highly respected theologians, deacons, pastors, preachers, and others of the cloth as well.

Thus when anti-Semitism rears its ugly head, and it is always just under the surface lurking around, the drums of hatred towards the Jew can be heard beating out the message of blaming the Jews for any and every ill that befalls a nation, a country and a community. History repeats itself because it seems in the Jew the world had found the perfect whipping boy. It has an entire people who, though usually with little or no political representation, through their own initiative and self-reliance have acquired sufficient wealth to be able to sustain themselves, and enjoy a prosperity that always seems to be the envy of all who cannot do as well.

The Jews were a people who were never allowed or who chose not to assimilate, and so it would seem a people that the empowered could safely blame, accuse, persecute; and as was so often the case down through recorded history, kill, murder, and destroy in every conceivable manner. They would always justify doing this by pointing out it was good riddance, and even necessary in most cases, for as those guilty of the killing of the Jews would point out, it says in the Bible that they are the ones responsible for killing Christ.

In some cases those very people actually doing the killing or just encouraging others to do so knew that nowhere in the Bible did it say that so-called Christians must take it upon themselves to make the Jewish people forever suffer for something they did not actually do. They remained quiet about it, and down through the ages this accusation has been hurled against people who for the most part were not able to defend themselves. The mass hysteria on behalf of their accusers has never been other than the mindless braying of fanatics showing the hate-motivated mindset of a murderous mob. They always had an ax to grind because a Jew was able to prosper, no matter where he was found, and was thus looked upon as an evil in league with the Devil.

How else could they be so prosperous, when all around them the real German people were so desperate? Thus it was that the Jew was to be just barely tolerated, even though they were usually well educated. They were the shop owners, but as a matter of necessity down through time, they were the ones the Protestants and the Catholics turned to for loans. They were very frugal, smart and able to manage money. They produced doctors, lawyers, pharmacists and other persons of status.

They accomplished all of this under a great handicap, kept their great faith in and love for God always elevated and highly visible, and in all of this they were very steadfast. For the most part, they kept to themselves. For all this, still non-Jews felt they were not to be trusted. Look at how they dressed and the matter of how they wore their hair back then. They had a natural air of being detached and removed from the majority and by most, this was taken that they felt superior.

Intellectually they were, but in spite of what they have always contributed to the societies they were in, it was never enough. After all was said and done, there was always that stigma that their kind had killed our Christ.

It was sad, but this played right into Hitler's plan. He was overjoyed to discover the existence, right here in America, of a made-to-order opportunity whereby through certain worthless promises he could make to the leaders of this world religious order – that of becoming the official religion of the world subject to the bloody Axis being victorious, of course – he could secure their own promise to sell out this country to the Nazis.

Call it naught but treason. Hitler found his opening, and realizing the enormous asset and advantage this bunch of traitors would be to him, meant to have them in place and doing his dirty work, all for an empty promise.

He knew them as fools. These were the very same misguided, fatally flawed, deadly ambitious and greedy seekers of power and glory at all costs that the Nazis would finance. As a certain radio commentator in this country was given to say about issues of vital importance that he would bring to our attention, "Now you've heard it, and now you know."

What should America be doing about it? That said, this brings us back to the battle between these two Olympians. On the one side the Great General American Land Company was taking on that great religious body, who they said were made up of angels and saints right here on Earth.

Sure they were.

While relatively new to our local community, they were maneuvering into a position of offense, having, as they felt, been cowardly attacked by the aforementioned Great General American Land Company and the dreaded but cowardly Ku Klux Klan that was controlled by this big old land company.

Now this was happening there in the Bootheel, on our County Line Road situated as it was in Southeast Missouri. Talk about poor timing; all this bad blood had surfaced just when the new township of Gobler was holding, for the first time ever, our very own County Fair, hosted by our good friend, the well-known and much-loved – though in many ways mysterious and sometimes strange – Mr. Denny Mitchell.

Unbeknownst to any of us, he was fighting several demons of his own at that time, about which I have already written. As it turned out, he was involved in some things so terrible as to be causing him to go through a complete reversal of all that he had been lending himself to. In a desperate effort to reclaim his self-respect, and to get right with God and man, he had embarked on a mission. The first step he had taken towards this end was at last to confide in his wife, who knew something was wrong, but not knowing what, was shocked when she learned what had been bothering her husband. In reality, she was forced to think the unthinkable: her husband was in the employ of the Nazis.

The second thing he did was to confess, in a manner of speaking, his great sin to my dad and uncle. We saw that he was genuinely sorry and desperate to make amends. He explained how he had gotten into the mess he was in. The coming of his brother who had escaped to this country, having been held captive along with the rest of his family in Ireland by the Nazis, brought Mr. Denny the heart-breaking revelation that his relatives were dead.

There was no longer any need for Mr. Denny to subject himself to the blackmail he had been under for the last several years. He no longer had to do exactly what his brother's captors demanded of him. There was no one left in Ireland for them to execute. As hard as it was for

Mr. Denny to accept that all his relatives in Ireland had been murdered, he could see that his own situation had changed. He had already decided before his brother turned up that he would throw off their yoke of threats and fears, and now he had one family member alive who by some miracle was here safe with him. Having now what had been a missing part of his plan, the securing of his family, he was ready to make a stand.

Then came the radio news that brought about a feeling of sickening paranoia – those killers were already here and were most certainly coming after his brother. The Nazis felt his brother knew too much, and they could not afford to let him live. There was too much at stake for this particular man to remain alive; he could alert the authorities as to what they were really doing. While Denny was not sure that they would try to kill him and his family, he knew for sure they were coming for his brother, and he was not going to let that happen.

What a royal mess. It was not enough that he had already been marked as one to whom the Klan would need to pay another, and more instructive, call. Now without any doubt, somewhere there were also killers making their way towards this very place, and he did not know what they looked like, if they were already here, and how many they were.

For with this fair there were so many more people here, most of them strangers. He was in trouble, of this there could be no doubt. He truly regretted that he had already endangered the Wiltshires. Mercy me, what a mess. Somehow, he could not help but feel that they would help him, and he sure needed help.

What was interesting to Denny was even though his problems seemed to be mounting, he felt free, more so than he had in several years. Yes, free to do what he knew was right. Though he was not the first person to say so about troubles and the like, as he was enjoying breathing the sweet fresh air of freedom right now, as far as those other dangers, be they close or far away, well, he would worry about them tomorrow.

If indeed, they could wait until tomorrow.

One thing that can always be counted on is that eventually, tomorrow becomes today. All those yesterdays will forevermore be fixed in time, unchangeable other than as our memories of them fade and become blurred. Some things, however, have such great importance that in retrospect, we can see clearly that as a result of certain events our lives were changed forever.

Without a doubt, World War II was just such an event, for we as a nation lost our innocence. We could no longer believe that we were protected by living between two great oceans. Time and distance were brought into a sharper prospective, and we were forced to acknowledge that we were vulnerable to many different dangers.

In our case, we were vulnerable to dangers both from within and without. From the first part of 1941 on through and including the middle of 1944, the news was, almost without exception, gloomy. The war was not going well for America, and what made it so bad for us farming people was that our favorite radio announcers, like Gabriel Heatter, had the kind of voices that by their very nature sounded sad. It was thought that he could announce that we had won the war and make it sound uneventful and sorrowful. But his delivery was cheerful when compared to our second most listened to news broadcaster, H. V. Kaltenborn, because he would come right out and announce first words out of his mouth,

"Ah, there's no good news tonight!"

Then he would tell us how bad the war was going, and we would just be brought down almost to the point of despair. Had not the Amos and Andy show come right after to cheer us up – which all of America listened to – I really believe that these two broadcasters alone, without intending to, could have totally demoralized America.

They served up gloom and doom so thick you could cut it with a knife, but theirs was just the tonic we seemed to need. Without exception, we could not wait to tune in to hear their weekly newscast.

It seemed we were gluttons for punishment. They were very much like members of our own family. They kept us informed and centered on world events as they unfolded around us. In addition, we had news coming to us through the voice of Edward R. Murrow from London. Sometimes the Germans were actually bombing that city as he spoke.

Can you imagine all this, in those dark and uncertain days of World War II?

In contrast to the dreariness of these three much respected announcers, we had last but not least the totally upbeat voice of Walter Winchell as he would always open his program with a cheerful, "Good, Mr. and Mrs. North and South America and all the ships at sea, let's go to press!" He did this to the sound of either a ticker-tape or a typewriter in the background. Then he would lift our spirits by telling us about things going on in Hollywood. Who was seen at certain parties and with whom? He had the ability to bring us into what was happening in places like New York, Chicago, Los Angeles, and so on. His was really a gossip program and most of what so thrilled us about what he had to say was pure conjuncture. He never told us anything definite, but the way he told us made us all transcend away from our merger existence.

During that short fifteen minutes of escapism, we could almost rub elbows with the stars. We took real comfort in feeling that regardless of how bad our troubles were, there was something better going on out there. We knew because Winchell told us so. My brother, sister and I could not wait to get out there and see for ourselves.

Shortly we would, and this great new awakening for all of us would begin as my story concludes itself.

Ch. 22: The Fair Winds Down

Let us return to the moment before I broke away to give further clarification to the extent of and the nature of the political situation on our County Line Road, and indeed the world in general at that time. Recall how Morley inadvertently and in an almost casual manner had finally mentioned to his dad and his uncle what he had seen that last night. He did this in an off-hand manner, at the last possible second as they were preparing to open the fair that morning, thus saving their lives as explosive devices had been rigged to go off when the front door opened.

Then came the extreme events of the day itself, some probable and others improbable. They all had to be sorted out and dealt with, the notable horse race held for the very first time on Mr. Denny's regulation five-mile long racetrack where one of his horses, won big time, Fleet Foot. Remember that he had two entered in that field of twelve. The other one took off running the wrong way, in the direction of the bog when the starter pistol fired – yes, that had happened on that very day. Then came the dilemma of the swamp gas, our search for Bob Tail in the night, and almost being bogged down in that quicksand ourselves.

The day was a big success in spite of the fact that the night before, the Klan had gathered to burn crosses in front of Mr. Denny's house. They probably would have burned his house too, except that a disaster befell the motley group of fellow terrorists as several of their vehicles suddenly and unaccountably burst into flames during that cool and frosty night. The Grand Wizard wrecked his car and almost killed himself as he sped away into the night from the whole thing.

One thing was for sure, there was no longer any doubt in Mr. Denny's or his brother's mind as to whether or not those assassins were here. They were. Not only did they have those fools to contend with but those who called themselves Klansmen were beginning to be a pain in the butt as well.

These solid citizens looked silly running around in the late afternoon, early evening, and late night wearing those perfectly good sheets that had been ruined by having cut those holes in them like they did. It should not come as a surprise that these boneheads would take themselves as seriously as it sadly appeared they did. One must keep in mind that these old boys thought of themselves as superior. For them, they felt it came with the territory of being white, and woe to any white person who did not recognize that superiority by the way they talked or acted towards the black man. They thought of such a person as uppity and an enemy of their state of mind. Such a person was hated more so than they hated the black man himself.

In our two counties there was not the first black man or Jew, and because of the nature of these men and their overriding need to hate someone, though not anyone who could fight back, mind you, these cowards made it their business to seize upon the third best bet – the poor farmer, especially us share croppers.

The Great General American Land Company used these ignorant, soul-destroyed bottom feeders of humanity – who can only be described as the suck-ups of all time – to keep us down and in line. In return, they basked in the warmth of the approval of this land giant who controlled everything down there on that County Line, from womb to tomb.

They were truly a sorry bunch of cheap-shot, morally bankrupt, despicable, wretched bloodsuckers. If ever there were such, then this bunch from towns around us surely were.

Lest I digress too far, I should explain that there was beginning to be a noticeable change in the tone of the news. For one, in their same serious delivery they were saying, especially H. V. Kaltenborn, "Ah, America, there is good news tonight."

It seemed the direction of the war was changing in our favor.

Oh, how sweet this news was to all of us loyal Americans, and it did not take long for this bunch who dressed themselves in the purple and white of religious royalty to realize how badly they had miscalculated. They chose to sell out this country in favor of backing those insane lunatics, the tintype dictators – the fanatical Fascists of Germany and Italy and, of course, the emperor-worshipping ones from Japan. They were the Axis who felt they were destined to be the rulers of the world. Can you imagine the world divided into three spheres of control under the sole dictatorship of these three men, Hitler, Benito, and Tojo, the Supreme Warlord of Japan?

How bitter their disappointment must have been, as through the grace of God that was not going to happen.

Ch. 23: A Sandstorm Hits

As to what did happen, we will start with the morning of the fourth day of our fair. The day broke with an orange sky, cold and blustery. That, in and of itself, did not bode well for the fair. There then proceeded to swoop down upon us a very damaging storm, which was unusual for us. It caused everything to come to a screeching halt. Everyone tried to protect his or her livestock. By necessity, the storm forced most all to remain inside, where we busied ourselves with trying to keep the sand and dust out of our houses.

It got in anyway, and ended up in our beds, our flour and meal bins, and everything else that was not covered up tight. We had never seen such as this, but we heard about the terrible dust storms that years back had done much damage in Oklahoma.

This was scary; we could not breathe. It was terrible and when the storm finally blew itself out, we came to discover that several amongst us had suffocated. We also came to grips with the awareness that this dust storm left us a new landscape, with dust by the ton in and on everything as far as the eye could see. The sand shattered windows and ruined all painted surfaces beyond repair. Wagons, old cars and trucks as well as combines and hay bailers were scraped down to bare metal in many cases.

It was a bad storm and it, like almost every other disaster that befell us, came without warning. So too would the terrible calamity that would visit itself upon us the following day, the fifth and final day of our grand fair.

On this day, or what was left of it, as the sandstorm subsided, the people camped out at Gobler busied themselves with making ready for a hasty departure. That pretty well signaled that our fair was at its end. Not officially mind you, as that would come tomorrow and we were counting on tomorrow as a time in which we could fully assess our storm damage. It was considerable, but it was as nothing compared to what was going to come down on us.

By about ten o'clock the next morning the wind was up again and the day got off to a cold start. Some heavy hail had begun to drop, lots of it, big marble-size hail that would have destroyed the crops if there had been any in the fields. Fortunately, all the crops had been gathered, and anything left standing was pretty much beaten down and partially covered by the great brownish-black towering columns of Oklahoma dust brought over and blasted into us by the previous day's storm.

Now it was hail being driven by the wind, and it was cold too. It sounded like all the furies of Hades were beating on every tin roof around, especially for those of us who had sought shelter in that road culvert. It was not yet put in the ground. It was just lying in the ditch like it was, but several of us boys on our way down to try and pick up some trash, with the added hope of finding something useful left behind when the people broke camp at the fair ground, sought cover in that rather old, corrugated road culvert. It was from there, looking out the end of that tube, that we saw the tornado. It was a giant of nature and carried with it devastation the likes of which only an act of God can produce.

As the twister came roaring by, it began to sling out boards and picket fence staves of purple and white. There fell on and around us dry goods, canned goods, cloth of different colors, some still trailing from the bolts. We knew that had come from the old Company Store. Mismatched shoes, brand new overalls, and several sheets fell from the sky. Something that looked like wet, misty flour covered our faces and got in our eyes and mouth, collecting around our nostrils. It had been slung in so quickly and the change in our appearance was so sudden and drastic that we could not help but laugh to look at each other.

As we looked from the end of that culvert out to the storm, there came more stuff that tasted – well, I cannot describe it as anything but awful.

It was not a fine, white slick salve anymore because this later mist came in the color of brown and stunk. We were no longer laughing. Then came a church tower with the bell still hanging on, which bonged and bonged as it tore asunder upon being slammed into our shelter. It bent that old culvert nearly in half. We all thought we were goners for sure.

It seemed as though the twister would never pass. It was at least a football field wide and seemed to touch down about an eighth of a mile in front of us, crossing the very ditch where we were hiding from it, and stopping. The hail stopped as well and it began to rain. It rained hard, but the rain did not make quite as much noise, and we thought that at least we could hear ourselves think.

Then we realized that with the rain we now had to deal with an equally dangerous problem. The ditch was beginning to fill up with water, and that brought with it the unmistakable smell and physical signs of someone's outhouse, and every house had one before the twister hit. This was fast turning into an ugly situation.

After what seemed like an eternity, that monster began to move on down towards Gobler. The stinking water was up to our chins.

As the sky was no longer roaring like the world gone mad, though it was still raining, we felt like the danger had passed. We began to venture forth from our refuge to see the devastation. Anxious parents looking for their children would shortly join us. My dad and mother had made it to our storm shelter along with my brother, sister and uncle.

About twenty minutes later, Dad and Uncle found us. We had not left and the water had begun to recede. We were all just sitting on the culvert in a kind of daze. Nothing looked the same. We sure did not look the same. When Dad finally came up to us, the way we looked caused him to be a little startled. We were all right, but we were about the only thing that was.

As a matter of fact, nothing was the same. The power

base of that church body was gone, ripped up, and hurled away. Some of it was on the road, the rest in the ditch, desecrated by the contaminated water it had come in contact with when it slammed most disrespectfully into the road and the ditch. Less than an hour ago, it was thought by many to be the grandest looking church – or according to some the gaudiest looking church – in all of Southeast Missouri.

More than that, though, before taking the church, the tornado leveled those neatly arranged, nicely grouped, new constructed purple and white ticky-tacky church-built and owned houses. It destroyed those same houses that a few days prior had been moved into by what we thought to be the friendliest people we had seen.

Ch. 24: The Gobler Nazis Disappear

Those stragglers we met as we were turning homeward, or at least the direction where our homes had been, those same people showed not the least sign of any of that aforementioned friendliness. This storm and the destruction it wrought had at the same time ripped the mask off these hypocrites, and their true colors were now showing. We did not know it then, but we would learn that not only were they without a church, but they had been abandoned by their *monsignor*.

Either he had chosen this time of almost total confusion to disappear, or the tornado had settled his hash. One way or the other we never saw him again. Inasmuch as it was no longer possible to deny that for the Nazis the war was all but lost, suddenly there was no longer any reason to keep up this elaborate pretense. The church was gone with only a few cinder blocks to be seen strewn around here and there, and not a single ticky-tacky four room purple and white prefab house was left standing.

All were gone in only three to four minutes, and though not as quickly but very shortly thereafter, all the abandoned faithful were to be seen leaving our area any way they could, disorganized and on foot. They no longer functioned as a well-organized body, but more like stragglers and displaced persons leaving a war zone.

While the storms had taken their toll on these seekers of the New Zion, during this time, though not to any storm, we also lost Mr. Denny Mitchell, his brother, and his son Morley.

The battle where it was believed they died must have been horrific. The morning of the tornado found them having cornered three of the German contingent in Mr. Denny's huge corrugated store and warehouse. There Mr. Denny and his brother surprised the Germans who had taken advantage of the distraction of the storm to set up the final death trap that would finish their business in Southeast Missouri, once and for all.

They did not figure that anyone in their right mind, other than saboteurs such as themselves, would be out in this storm. They worked in a careless manner, leaving the front door ajar, for instance. I reckon from their first attempt to kill Mr. Denny that they had fashioned a key, so this time they just let themselves in the front door as big as you please. The Mitchells, upon seeing the door ajar as they approached the entrance, had the element of surprise on these jokers.

Mr. Denny kept two shotguns, both double barreled and loaded, out of sight in the store. They must have very quietly made their way to where they were hidden. We will never know for sure about the details of it. All we know is that as a result of the sandstorm the day before, Mr. Denny's truck would not start, so they rounded up the horses, Fleet Foot and Myrt. It must have been terrible riding with the storm raging as it was.

Something must have given them away. Once they were inside the store, a gunfight broke out. With the hail peppering the roof and side of that huge corrugated warehouse, those Germans might well have become unnerved, having managed to get that great explosive device in place. They probably feared it going off by the slightest jarring, even the heavy thunder and hail banging on the building. They turned tail and fled outside, grabbing the first two horses they saw.

That would have been old Myrt, a bad choice, and Bob Tail. I do not know when he had come up, but it seemed the fleeing Germans mounted two on one, one on the other, and dashed wildly into the interior of the swamp. Myrt, being a very smart old girl, was not having any of this and refused to go past a certain point. When she stopped, Bob Tail stopped.

Naturally these three members of the master race, seeing that these two steeds were of no use to them, got off, and proceeded on foot. Being all but blinded by the hard driving hail, they proceeded right into the quicksand and were stuck.

They were stuck there, alone and with no help forthcoming. They were shortly pulled under, flailing and screaming all to no avail. The last thing they heard, if indeed this was the way it had happened, was the explosion of their rigged bomb, the one that they had managed to get in place and set to go off if jarred or disturbed in any manner.

If the Germans were in the bog and able to hear the explosion, all things considered, it probably was not much of a comfort to them. It did explode and it took the lives of three of the heroes of our story – Mr. Denny, his son and his brother – thus wiping out the last surviving male members of the Mitchell Family.

It could have happened like that. We found the place where three people died, totally demolished. It was thought that enough explosive material was used to do the job five times over. What was left was only a wasted place of twisted steel. The explosion set the place on fire. Practically everything inside burned, as did the bodies identified as the Mitchells, all burned beyond recognition and blown to pieces.

Nothing was left to identify any of them, so everyone just naturally assumed these were the remains of Mr. Denny, his son and his brother. It is for sure that Myrtle was not going to tell any tales, nor was Bob Tail or Fleet Foot. As for the Nazis sucked down into that quicksand, if indeed they were, they would shed no light on anything either. In truth, they had disappeared along with several hundred others, all in one way or another, shortly following the last two devastating days of the one and only County Fair the township of Gobler would ever host.

With the tornado, the rains would last for the better part of two weeks and bring us flood conditions that only came about every four or five years. This flood and the storm that came with it would be especially dreadful, and though Mrs. Mitchell took over what was left of the store – it was not much – she tried for about a month or so to start rebuilding it. All she could do was get it partially cleared away. She did not keep at it long, as it was hopeless.

Over time, the waters receded. It was as if the entire Bootheel of Southeast Missouri were under water. People had to get out to high ground any way they could. It was a complete disaster, and it took the poor people of our County Line Road years to recover.

Many never did.

With two great storms coming as they did within a two-day period, we were already overburdened. We were all poor and without resources with which to recover. That alone would have been the end of our security, little as it was. With this great flood coming on the heels of that, well it proved to deliver the knockout blow.

The rains came day after day and we watched, as water got higher until it finally covered our porches and came into the houses. Those who would be there, quite a few because of having no way to get their meager belongings out, found themselves trapped. In desperation to save themselves, they tried to swim, float out on rafts or get out in flat bottom boats. Those that did get out made their way to Kennett, Deering, or any other safe haven they could find.

Those were desperate times, to be sure. No, the federal government did not declare it an emergency; there was no help from any source. The water would hang around for weeks. I do not know how anyone survived. My family had already loaded up our newly acquired old ton and a half Chevrolet truck, found Route 66 and was safely in California.

Well, we were in a work camp in Brawley.
We were later told that when the water began to recede, things slowly began to dry out. The water had returned to the Mississippi and finally the sea, and had taken almost all the gravel and dirt that had been hauled in to fix up our County Line Road as well as the other roads graveled as well as paved. They said the damage was total.

How fortunate we were to have gotten out when we did.

They told us that there was a constant stink everywhere of rotting fish that died, not being able to escape back to deeper water. They were left behind in low places like cornrows, ditches, and fast-disappearing puddles left in countless pastures. Some died on porches and in barns.

That abundance of rotting fish produced a plague of rats, which prompted the county to come out as soon as the flood conditions would allow. They gave shots of one kind or another, and not all thought it was a good thing. Quite a few of the old people flat out refused, saying that the government did not care about helping them when they needed help. They accused them of being there to kill them with shots. People as a whole did not trust the government any longer, and several of the crusty old people told them what they could do with their needles and such.

However, over time, slowly, the racetrack began to revert back to its natural state. As for the store, since it had only partially been cleaned up and there was no longer a driving force behind its rebuilding, the adventure was lost. It was gone forever along with any romance that at one time was associated with it. A few of the locals who remained and a few others, who were curious, would make their way down to what remained and walk around. Every now and again, they would just shake their heads. Some said that every year at fair time, a very clear, distant pealing of many, delightful sounding bells fell happily on the ears of some people who would still be down there listening, listening even after all the time that had passed.

Now it went without saying that it was a hard life, especially for a woman alone as Mrs. Mitchell was – she never remarried. She finally had enough and she too pulled up stakes and left the County Line forever. That was some time after we had left. In our case, we saw the writing on the wall. The Great General American Land Company had suffered losses, and they were many. It survived and was still in operation. Before the great flood, it had purchased new farming equipment, cotton picking machines to be exact, that could do in one day what thirty people did in a week.

We could see that we were going to be ousted, even though we were one of the few families who had not accepted the bogus offer that religious body had dangled in front of us. In addition, too many bad memories and drastic changes would continue to come, making us obsolete. Our back-breaking labor was no longer in demand, so we knew our usefulness was at an end.

My dad managed to buy an old Chevy truck. We fitted it with bows on the back, over which we stretched a heavy tarp, and loaded onto it all we owned. We struck out for California, searching for Route 66 and the promised land that Walter Winchell told us about.

We found it, but that is for another story.

As for this story, the sad saga of the Mitchell Family, I hope you have noticed that while we all had reason to believe that the Mitchell men were dead, I have cast an element of doubt. It could have been possible that the three unidentifiable bodies in the burned-out warehouse and mercantile store were in reality the three assassins – that they had set off that explosion prematurely and killed themselves instead.

That would mean that there were no bodies in the bog, and when the explosion went off, the Mitchell men were not there as yet. Upon hearing the explosion, they would have felt the concussion from it. They would have been at least four miles away at the time they felt the jolt. It was at that time that the storm was letting loose with all its fury. Fortunately, they were still out on that old, bad road, battling the worst storm they had ever seen while trying to reach Gobler.

When they finally arrived and saw the total ruin and sparse remaining body parts of what they agreed were once three people, they would have decided this to be the perfect time to stage their own demise, seeing that none of the remains could be identified.

Oh, at first they probably experienced complete despair. Slowly, they would have begun to see in this a certain opportunity for themselves. They could use this wreck and ruin as a way to escape. They had so many enemies – the Klansmen that still sought to finish their lesson to teach the uppity Denny Mitchell a lesson or two about the danger that would befall any and everyone who would get cross with the Klan, as he had done. Lord only knew who else.

It is possible that they then could have planned this disappearing act with the full knowledge and complicity of Mrs. Mitchell. She would join them later at a predetermined place and time. Do not forget that Mr. Denny had cleaned up on the race and still had lots of the Nazis' money. With the two great storms coming back to back and the torrential rains that hung around for days, it would appear that this provided them just the opportunity to disappear without notice.

It is a theory.

I do know that Bob Tail did show back up, and that those three beautiful animals the Mitchells owned were seen being loaded into a rather large covered truck late one night, about a week after the terrible disaster. Someone said that the person taking them looked a lot like Morley, but you know how people are about starting stories and such. Besides, it was dark when this supposedly took place.

It is worth noting, though, that Mrs. Mitchell did not report her horses missing, even though the three had not been seen since the reported sighting of them being loaded into a truck. It is worth pondering. If it is true, then it is not any stranger than what happened to Hitler, Benito, and the Supreme Warlord of Imperial Japan, Tojo.

For those of you who may, by chance, be reading this and for whatever reason do not know what happened to those three would-be world dictators, I think you would find it very interesting. Get on your computer there, and you may be able to see just how serious were the times that I have written about. Find out about rural America as it was during the 1940's, and perhaps you can better appreciate the perils that we who lived through it had to face.

Then you will know more of what I was trying to say as I made an honest attempt to capture the spirit of those times, as seen through the eyes of the Wiltshires' youngest son and those whose lives I have attempted to capture on paper while telling of the sad saga of the Mitchell Family.

You may wonder what happened to certain of the people featured, sometimes rather prominently, in this story.

There were, for instance, those two old recluse men from whom Mr. Denny bought the swampland, who he had come to believe were in reality German agents. When it became obvious the war could not be won by Germany, acting on orders they received from the Captain of that mysterious submarine, they quickly packed up that transmitter and quietly abandoned that old, crude lean-to that had served as their base of operations for several years. They made tracks to rendezvous with the submarine in the hope of a safe return to Germany, but alas, that was never to be. They managed to get aboard the sub, but it sank in less than three days on its way back to the Fatherland. These blind fools had sacrificed everything, including their lives, all for nothing. They had lived like rats, and in the final act, they had died like rats, trapped on the submarine that had been their lifeline to the Fatherland lo those many years.

Their Fuehrer had failed, Germany had failed, the sub had failed, and finally they too failed and died. For what? For some sick, demented, so-called Fuehrer whose only real accomplishment was that through his madness, he managed to build the world's most successful killing machine. In doing so, he murdered wantonly on a scale that staggers the imagination. Who did he have murdered by the millions?   Why the defenseless Jew, naturally. It is sad, but true.

Then there is the one who was a real, live hero, our own Mr. Barlow Skinner. Barlow had nothing going into this story, other than the one thing the cowardly lion wanted most of all when Dorothy met him in "The Wizard of Oz." He wanted courage, and though Barlow had nothing else, he had courage. Though injured and burned badly of face and body, hurt and humiliated by his tormentors, he single-handedly took on the Klan and beat them at their own game. He had succeeded such that their effectiveness as a terror group was all but over.

Mr. Barlow Skinner survived and ran for Sheriff of Dunklin County. By beating all the odds, he won. Everyone who would come to know Sheriff Skinner, it seems, would have nothing but respect for Barlow the Man. He held the position until he died, about seven years later.

I have to say, I am proud of him. Barlow was loved. Inasmuch as this is the story of the sad saga of the Mitchell Family, with smatterings of the Wiltshires thrown in, I can say that this story could just as well be about Barlow Skinner as well, from his sad beginnings to the sadder ending to his life. He had overcome tremendous odds only to die in that infernal swamp. I for one am glad that he had those good years as Sheriff.

He accomplished more than any of the rest of us. He was a hero, and I do hope, dear reader, that you come to know and love Barlow Skinner, Sheriff of Dunklin County in Southeast Missouri from 1944 to 1951. He was the sheriff that carried an old Ronson cigarette lighter that did not work, because of being out of flint. His gun did not work either, because of his refusal to put bullets in it. Though he was badly scarred and limped some, he was able to do his job as sheriff very well. He looked very smart in his khaki uniform, topped off with his ridged tan-colored Stetson hat, and complimented by his shiny brown patent leather dress shoes. Add the pair of World War II bomber pilot sunshades he wore and that shiny, silver, slightly oversized badge to his tailored shirt, well, he looked great.

He was well loved by everyone thereabout, knew all the

people by their last names, and called the young ones by their first. When certain of the children would be afraid of him because of the way he looked, scarred and all, he was known to take them on his knee, let them feel his badge, and, removing his hat, would invite them to touch his scared face to see that this would not hurt them. They would no longer be afraid of him, or at least not as much as before and in truth, he had such a gentle way with the children. It was not long after first meeting Mr. Barlow Skinner that they seemed to disregard his disfigured conditioned. They were able to see that he was a very nice man, and in spite of how he looked, he was a very gentle man, as well.

He was the perfect one for the job of sheriff, since he had quelled the Klan on that one cool and frosty night back when. They never were aware as to who it was that damn near burnt them out. They just had a taste of their own medicine and it was enough to let them know that burning things up was a game that could be played by others than just themselves. They had asked many a one, "Did you see who done it?"

Now for the time of irony, the one who these cowards feared most, because they did not know who had done it, was now the Sheriff. He knew all about these "night riders," who they were, where they lived. He knew every one of them and was able to keep an eye on them. He was able to curtail their activities simply by showing up where they were planning their next mischief.

There were a few die-hard Klansmen lurking about, but for the most part, they were finished. Law and order came with the election of Mr. Barlow Skinner as Sheriff. Though he had to learn all the techniques of law enforcement, from the beginning it was hard and he took his job very seriously.

What was more; the people who elected him were backing him in his attempt to clean up the county. With the war all but over, even the Klan could see that the times, they were a-changing. Their day of power through intimidation, threats, lynching, tarring and other terror tactics was no longer the fashion. They were finished.

With them believing that their last dragon needed slaying, Mr. Denny Mitchell had been blown to smithereens along with his son and foreigner brother – this story was repeated often enough that it was accepted as truth – there was really no longer, in their way of thinking, any opponents worthy of the Klan's attention.

Thus this fizzling bunch of terribly misguided, would-be killers of those who would challenge the status quo in that back water of Southeast Missouri faded away and ceased acting in the Klan's name. They surfaced again as businessmen and leaders in their respective churches. As far as anyone could determine, no one was ever charged with a crime. It was like a new dawn, and people seemed only too happy to let bygones be bygones.

So it was, and this brings to a close what I saw as the sad saga of the Mitchell Family. It is sad in that everyone thought they had died in that horrible explosion. Certainly, the bits and pieces of the remains of three men had to be accounted for.

It is a puzzle, one I fear the answer to has yet to become clear. Sheriff Skinner said that he would find out, even if it killed him. Indirectly, it did. He was to drain the swamp in the fall of 1951. That was when he died, or at least when he disappeared poking around in that swamp. He was alone. It was said that the bog got him, and if he did cry out, there was no one to hear.

October 1951 was the end of an age and the end of his life and all too short career. It was also the end of our way of having existed, year after year, down through time. We knew it as often brutal, sometimes kind. As I have stated, there was just barely a living to be made by us who were living out lives out there on the old County Line.

When we finally heard about his death, we had already left California by that time and lived about a year in Missouri and Arkansas before moving to Texas, where we've stayed since 1947. I remember Dad saying, when he heard about this death, that he was not so sure that was that.

He felt Barlow was too smart to be caught in that quicksand, and since he never carried a loaded pistol, what got him was probably a cat. There were at least two big, blue-black panthers in there, maybe more. Those full-grown carnivores weighed about eighty to ninety pounds.

With Barlow down there in that swamp by himself, probably stooping and kneeling around while in that bog, he would have been an irresistible meal to those stalkers. Having the element of surprise in their favor, they would have attacked without warning, and it would have all been over in less than a minute. Then they would have drug his body off somewhere nearby, after covering it with brush leaves and dirt.

They would have left it and retired somewhere not too far away, where they could keep an eye on it. Over the next couple of days, they would have gorged themselves of their kill.

They would finally have to carry the remains up to a large kill tree, where they would guard it with ease, because from the advantage of their lofty position, they could see every challenger as they approached.

As Dad said that is probably how it was; nothing personal in any of it, it was just nature's way. Uncle said those big cats probably made their living off the animals that came to drink at the swamp, and he was right; someone later reported they had found what they believed to be the remains of deer as well as what was determined to be human remains. At least two such bodies were found. One of them was thought to have been black, though that was very strange as it was believed there had been no black people in our vicinity other than several of those prisoners.

It was remembered that one had escaped and had never been found, perhaps until now. The other was

Caucasian, still with definite signs of having been burned during his life. Found there too was an old cigarette lighter.

Perhaps it was Barlow Skinner.

They found the lighter under a large sweet gum tree. High, about half way up, they found the two human remains and strange, but true, only a short distance away, an old honey tree full of fresh honey.

For whoever it was that was killed by those big black cats, it was their end. It is likewise the end of this story. I hope that you have enjoyed my recollections of the sad saga of the Mitchell Family, as happened long ago and far away.

Looking back, I think it is safe to say, "Weren't we a bunch?"

Robert S. Wiltshire, 2005

Dedication: Bob Wiltshire Presents This Book To His Family

As the years rolled by and I became a man, I spent every waking moment in love with and in awe of the beauty of our time, of our world as we came to know it. I was, all the while, in pursuit of a wonderful life; and I found it.

I found that – for which I had been looking – about which so much has been written, and much more, with the wonderful woman who did me the great honor of marrying me, thus saving me from myself. She became the mother of our four remarkable children.

Truly my cup has been overflowing, and now I honestly know what the word "wonderful" implies. Each time I hear one of my children say, " Hi, Dad"; "Goodbye, Dad"; "We've missed you, Dad"; or "I love you, Dad," now, to me, that is wonderful.

My late wife would feel that way too. So if you are listening, Hon, we miss you, we love you, we need you, and we always will. Thus, my dear departed wife and my great children, my grandchildren, and great-grandchildren, this story is dedicated to you.

I'd like to take this time to pass some rosebuds around and say some things to my wonderful family that need to be said. It makes me feel good at my age just to be able to talk to them, even in my story. So there. I will say it again. Children, I love you. That is the truth. You can count on it.

And in the end I would say every single word of this story is "true" – I say yes – maybe not "factual," because those old facts can be kinda dry and sometimes even though you get them right, they don't convey the "truth" of the matter – but "true"? Oh yes, because each detail is meant to help convey the flavor of our life back then.

After all, it was no less than Mark Twain who told us that "faith" consists of "believing in something you just know ain't true." (from "The Adventures of Huckleberry Finn.")

That's where faith and imagination come in, and that's where real storytelling, which I've loved and engaged in all my life, begins and ends.

So I'll leave you, dear readers, with words from a favorite book of mine, "Peter Pan" by J.M. Barrie: "To live will be an awfully big adventure," and so it has been.

Tributes

By Regina Ramsey – I remember Daddy sitting at the center of our Christmas gatherings at Grandmother's house with everyone listening as he regaled us with stories of his youth. Our cousins, Pam in particular, would laugh and encourage him to continue, while his sister and our mother would give him the eyebrow that said, "Wrap it up, Mister…." And me? Well, I was bored to tears because I had heard the stories so many times before.

I was a foolish child. I had no idea, at the time, what a precious gift he was giving us. I had no idea, at the time, that he was teaching me how to tell a story. I had no idea, at the time, that one day he would be gone and there would be no more stories. But he didn't allow his voice to be silenced or his memories to fade out of our consciousness – no, he took the time to record it all, and now others can share in his stories too.

I feel sorry for those who will only read the words and never experience the true passion behind them. The way he would act out the dramatic parts with his hand motions and his thunderous voice, the facial expressions he used, the way he would pause for effect when he was about to deliver the climax. No one could tell a story quite like he could.

 I remember having friends over to visit and Daddy would sit us down at the table for dinner and he would assign a word for each of us to look up in the dictionary, then make us use it in a sentence. It would embarrass me no end, but he would go on to captivate my friends with his wonderful stories; and they would go on and on about how funny my dad was and how they wished he was their dad. It seems our dad was one of a kind and to my shame, these are childhood joys that I took for granted.

 It is only now that I am much older that I can truly appreciate the man he was. He was a man of little education, only having made it to the sixth grade, but that didn't stop him from educating himself; in fact, he was brilliant. The man read the dictionary literally every day, He would get so excited about the words he would find that he then, in turn, would force me to learn them too. He forged a passion in my brain for words, and they have carried me through life until this day.

 There are so many times that I hear him when I speak. Truthfully, it scares me a little, but by the same token, I take a strange source of pride in it. I see him in the words of my stories and I think, wow, who would I have been had I not been his daughter? I am thankful that his stories now have a chance to live on.

By Marissa Elliott: Let me tell you a story.

Those are the words I heard, Robert Wiltshire, my granddad, utter so many times. Those words would light up his face and make his blue eyes bluer. My Granddad was one of the greatest men I have ever known; and I will miss him very much. If there could be a perfect person to speak at this service, it would be my granddad without a doubt. He had a true gift for telling stories. He did not just tell stories, he transported the listeners to another time and place. He remembered details that the average person would overlook. When he was speaking, his audience would let their cold drinks become warm and their hot food become cold. He was that intriguing.

He lived a rich life, not in the monetary sense, but in the sense that he lived with a purpose and a passion. His purpose and his passion were people. He did not allow strangers to be strangers. He did not keep his warm smile reserved for special occasions, and that smile was contagious. He reached out to every person he met with a genuinely kind and humble approach. I don't believe he had a shy bone in his body. I remember watching him talk to the wait staff in restaurants and to nurses in the hospital. It did not matter how good or bad he was feeling, he would always want to know how the people around him were doing...what their situation was, were they having a good day? Those strangers, those perfect strangers, would always react to his kindness in the most amazing way. The hard lines on their faces would soften and the tone of their voice would get higher. They were suddenly at ease in his presence as though they had known him for as many years as I had. His kindness was a gift. God gave him this gift, and he shared it with everyone.

Sadly, I was not able to be there for his last moments on this earth, but I am certain that this is one thing that never changed about him. I know our family will miss him always; but I am comforted in the knowledge that this great man with such a loving spirit is now meeting up with Jesus and his beloved wife (my grandmother), Dolores Wiltshire, who passed too soon before him. I love you, Granddad.

Bob & Dolores Wiltshire

Young Love
Forever Love

About the Author:

By Sybrina Durant – Robert S. Wiltshire was born on a blustery, snowy day – thus he was christened with the middle name Snow. That's the story he always told, anyway. That little boy, who also had snow-white hair, soon became known as Bobby Snow to his family. He was a handful for his parents, especially his mother, who probably wondered at times if he'd make it to adulthood. His boyhood adventures were stressful enough to cause any mother's hair to turn gray real quick.

As Bobby got older he came to be known as Bob. Over the years, his signature hair color changed from blonde to brown and finally to gray. Fortunately, he did grow up and to his mother's delight he had a family of his own. Raising his offspring eventually stripped the color out of his own hair. But through all of the ups and downs each of his children always knew we were cherished, just as he knew the same of his parents.

Our Dad loved to regale – what we thought of as, his captive audiences – with wild and crazy tales. But the truth was, everyone loved to listen to his stories, egging him on at each twist and turn. Each was finely crafted to bring out a smile here and a belly laugh there. His greatest joy late in his life was seeing genuine smiles and hearing merry laughter from those people he loved most.

I wish he had lived long enough to become familiar with the Internet. What joy it would have given him to be able to find other writers still familiar with the people and places he wrote about. I'm certain he would have contacted everyone he could find for a chance to reminisce and hear how others remembered the unusual events of the times he wrote about.

This story was written by a 75-year-old man from his memories as a ten-year-old boy. Naturally, many of those memories may have been embellished over the years. I have done a lot of research while editing his book to try to find concrete evidence of the local events described herein. I must say that it has been a very difficult task to track down much of anything that is historically verifiable, and I'm left wondering how much of this story was simply meant to be a creative and entertaining endeavor and how much of it really did occur.

I've finally come to the conclusion that just about every bit of it must have been made up by that incorrigible Bobby Snow just for the fun of it. So I've left the names of the people and places intact. I had planned to change them to protect the innocent but in all actuality there's so much fantasy mixed in amongst such a very small amount of reality that I don't see how too much harm could be done to anyone's reputation after so many years.

Robert Wiltshire left this earth on June 25, 2011. I wish he had lived long enough to hold his very own novel in his hands.

Our home was full of books – books on every subject known to man were everywhere you looked. And he had read them all so many times he could quote long passages from them. It was his dream to be among the ranks of those other authors he regarded so highly.

When he was a youngster he didn't develop a love of reading at the same age other kids did. I think it probably was because when he was young he would just rather be doing something adventuresome outside than to be stuck inside reading about that adventure in a book.

When his family moved from Missouri to California, he discovered just how good some of those adventurous books actually were, and with the help of a few good-hearted people, he finally learned to read with a vengeance, steeping himself in some of those stories that surely changed the course of his life. During his young years he would have had the opportunity to read books like "Wings of the Navy," "War Wings," "Doomed Demons," all by Eustace L. Adams; John Prentice Langley's "Bridging the Seven Seas"; and "Four Aces" by Thomson Burtis. I can imagine, some of those books must have been the impetus for joining the Air Force later!

And mixed in with all the splendid war books were those typical boys' adventure books, mainly starring the Hardy Boys – I can remember him referring to "The House on the Cliff," "The Secret of the Old Mill," and "The Shore Road Mystery." It was some of these mysteries written for pint-sized folks that first got him interested in being a storyteller.

I wish he could show this memoir to everyone and proudly proclaim, "I wrote this!" I can just imagine his happiness at having accomplished such a thing. Bobby relished entertaining family and friends with stories from his past, and everyone loved to hear them over and over again. His joyful noise is sorely missed by all who knew him.

Information About The Editing Process:

By Sybrina Durant — I want to take a moment to give special thanks to the people who spent hours editing this book. I have to say, all I had to start with was a pdf file of scanned paper filled with the most unimaginably unreadable text. At the time that Bob was composing his story, he was also learning how to use a computer. I can't tell you how many times he lost his story files and had to start over.

Luckily he had printed out most of the book before he managed to finally destroy his computer by deleting files. When I asked him why he had deleted particular files, which just happened to be operating system files, he explained, "Well, I deleted everything that I didn't know what it was!" So there you have it. At that point, all I could do was grin and bear it…and get him a new computer. But alas, there were no further stories to be captured as he quickly succumbed to the ravages of dementia and Alzheimers.

Those scanned image files went to a very patient editor named Lynn Perretta. She went over the book with a fine tooth comb, untangling the mess into a very presentable form. I am grateful for her time and expertise.

I quickly realized that many details could be expanded upon for the reader's cultural edification. Happily, for that purpose, I came across another wonderful editor, Susan Seawolf Hayes. She spent countless hours thinking up the clever chapter titles and also rearranged the book format to make it more effortlessly flow. I asked her to include some additional details to ensure that this story came alive and truly brought to mind the flavor of the era. Through exhausting research, per my request, she ghosted in many fun and interesting facts about that time period that I hope you enjoy.

Both Lynn and Susan kept the voice of the author true to my Dad's. Finally, I want to thank my daughter, Marissa Elliott. She also spent many hours in the editing process and the Chapter 3 title was her idea.

More Information About Gobler, The Country Store And Other Stuff

http://kboa830.com/a-tribute-to-a-country-store/ - A Tribute to a Country Store, by Virginia B. Branch.

http://anniejoysletters.blogspot.com/2011/03/going-to-gobler-before-there-was.html - Short stories by Annie Joy.

https://books.google.com/books?id=TMphy5gc6aMC&printsec=frontcover&source=gbs_atb#v=onepage&q&f=false – Link to a book titled "Deering Plantation" by Ophelia R. Wade. It contains information about Denny Mitchell and also discusses the religious group that bought 5,000 acres in the area.

http://littlerivervalley.com/6/post/2013/11/more-this-and-that.html - Blog containing information about the Gobler Mercantile Store.

Interested in learning more about Sonja Henie?
http://www.biography.com/people/sonja-henie-9334831

Here's a song you might really like…it reminded me of Robert Wiltshire and his brother, Jack. – "In Color" by Jamey Johnson - https://youtu.be/EYGwxf1gCC4

Visit Sybrina.com for more books by Sybrina Durant and Gina Rose (Pen name for Regina Ramsey).

www.ingramcontent.com/pod-product-compliance
Lightning Source LLC
Chambersburg PA
CBHW020612120726
47905CB00003B/761